STONE MOUNTAIN

The stage robbery had been accomplished by an old woman. Twine Fourch had never heard of a female being a highway robber before. He followed the trail all the way to a dilapidated log cabin up Stone Mountain. What happened after that no one could believe even after townsmen from Jefferson found the old log house and the skeletal dying old woman. But before the mystery could be solved there would be two unnecessary killings, a bizarre suicide and a lynching.

Books by Concho Bradley
in the Linford Western Library:

THE FLATHEAD COUNTRY
DEVIL'S DEN

CONCHO BRADLEY

STONE MOUNTAIN

Complete and Unabridged

LINFORD
Leicester

First published in Great Britain in 1998 by
Robert Hale Limited
London

First Linford Edition
published 1999
by arrangement with
Robert Hale Limited
London

British Library CIP Data

Bradley, Concho, *1916* –
    Stone Mountain.—Large print ed.—
    Linford western library
    1. Western stories
    2. Large type books
    I. Title
    813.5′4 [F]

ISBN 0–7089–5490–1

Published by
F. A. Thorpe (Publishing) Ltd.
Anstey, Leicestershire

Set by Words & Graphics Ltd.
Anstey, Leicestershire
Printed and bound in Great Britain by
T. J. International Ltd., Padstow, Cornwall

This book is printed on acid-free paper

1

Manhunting

The founding of settlements west of the Missouri River followed similar, traditional patterns. The first requisite was water, the second, third and fourth requirements were miles of graze and browse country, timber, as much protection as was possible from fierce weather and, finally, some basis for trade, commerce and emigration.

The Jefferson settlement had most of the desirables. Eventually emigration and its companion, growth, would occur, but not before living off the land atrophied and that wouldn't be for several generations.

Until the ultimate requirement, the railroad, would condescend to lay track to Jefferson, the settlement remained not much different from other grass and water settlements in what had for centuries been the domain of the Indian.

The Indians were disappearing along with their mainstay, the buffalo, and the vast timbered uplands were being scarred with stumps of the trees necessary for buildings. The most striking feature of the area was a huge massif called Stone Mountain.

During some epochal period, probably not long after the earth cooled, what was a high, round dome was visited by some kind of cataclysm which sheared off most of the southern part of the mountain leaving two sunken places on either side of an out-thrust which defied destruction. The Indians, given as they were to naming everything, called it Eagle Mountain. There was a resemblance, not striking, but that lack was overcome by aboriginal imagination.

The latecomers to the territory with less imagination and spirituality called it simply Stone Mountain.

Stone Mountain overlooked all the southerly country. It was the highest eminence in the necklace of rims that quartered around from east to west forming an uneven but adequate shelter from the worst weather coming from the north.

The face of Stone Mountain overlooked hundreds of miles of grass country and the Jefferson settlement, where traders of different kinds had become established.

It was not a large settlement and it lacked some specific necessities such as a medical doctor, a preacher, an apothecary and other adjuncts of civilization, but there was a large emporium — general store — a smithy, a place to eat, a combination livery and public corral both of which were adjacent to the log office and corralyard of the stage company.

Jefferson's more recent acquisition included a gunsmith's which was also a silversmith's, and a stout log jailhouse out of what had originally been a fort where folks sheltered when the tribesmen went on a foray. The jailhouse was occupied by another late arrival, an individual named Twine Fourch, a large, powerful, unsmiling, taciturn man who wore his constable's badge in plain sight. His name was actually Antoine Fourché, his father having been a *voyageur*, mother a Shoshone woman who resided in a hide tipi which offered both privacy and protection against a fierce winter, a very long winter.

In the Stone Mountain country he was known as Twine Fourch and because ignorance is its own reward he accepted the mispronunciation because since childhood that was how his name was said.

In a raw country niceties are not important, survival is important. Twine Fourch got his job as lawman after a series of stage robberies prompted the Denver-based headquarters of the stage company to threaten to discontinue stage and light freight service to Jefferson.

4

After Twine's appointment to regional lawman, the stage robberies stopped and that inevitably occasioned a threatening rumour in a place without newspapers and where, therefore, gossip thrived.

Why should the robberies stop when Twine Fourch became the law? Because, being a 'breed of some kind, he was probably implicated. Half-bloods had been historically mistrusted and in many cases the mistrust was justified. Half-breeds were rarely accepted and if they were big, fearless and competent fighters with fists or weapons, mistrust was capable of becoming respect and mistrust.

Twine Fourch had friends, not many, and it was reasonable to assume some of those friends were influenced by intimidation. Twine Fourch was not talkative nor did he have to be. He was large, powerfully muscled, expressionless with unwavering, jetblack eyes.

He knew the Stone Mountain country

as well and probably better than anyone else. He had been born and raised in the shadow of Stone Mountain.

Stories about him abounded. It was said he had once been married, which was untrue. It was also said in his youth as a fighting Shoshone he had killed and scalped many men, which was also untrue. His mother and her people had been rounded-up and taken away by the army when he'd been small. An old 'breed trapper had taken him in and raised him. The old trapper was religious. Twine Fourch was not, at least to local knowledge. The question could have been satisfactorily resolved by a single question, but west of the Big River people didn't ask personal questions. It wasn't just bad manners, it could result in injury.

In Twine Fourch's case it didn't matter. All that mattered was that in four years of being the law he had proven his ability.

Until another stage was robbed.

It was the custom in areas devoid of

banks for people to cache their money. In Jefferson there was an alternative, the huge steel safe in the general store whose balding proprietor, Calvin Lott, had clawed his way to success and was not a good man to cross.

He was not as tall as Twine Fourch, but he was heavier and solid in his middle age. There were some things he did and some things he didn't; he sold only for cash on the barrel head, extended no credit and had a notorious temper. Among local rumours was one that Cal Lott was a widower and an army deserter. In fact, he had never been married and had been invalided out of the army during the War Between the States; he had been shot during a minor skirmish by a Rebel with better valour than eyesight. The musket ball had hit him a little east of the tail-bone. A soldier who couldn't march long distances or sit squarely on a bench was a detriment.

Cal Lott and Twine Fourch tolerated each other. It was not quite a friendship;

neither of them favoured close relationships and this situation was not helped when the latest coach hold-up cost Cal Lott a moneybox, not coming to him in Jefferson but going north to Denver from store profits. A solid year of profits.

Twine left Jefferson on the north-south coach road and with a minimum of difficulty located the place where the robbery occurred. The coach driver had hauled back on his binders making skid marks for a hundred feet.

It was the same boulder-strewn length of road other highwaymen had favoured and that fact suggested to Twine that the robber was familiar with the area. What shocked him was the description: the highwayman had been an old Indian squaw.

He found horse sign on the west side of the road where an animal had been tied among some sickly pine trees.

There were other signs; the best one was in the soft soil of the westerly roadside berm. Boot tracks fresh and plain as day.

He wasted no time looking for anything else. Big men rode stout horses. Twine's animal had little piggy eyes, a dark streak down his back — the sign of a buckskin animal — and had been shod recently. Gnarled nail-heads, eight to a shoe, showed where the lawman's animal left sign among boulder fields.

The highwayman's tracks were also of a horse recently shod, with smaller hooves than Twine's buckskin and with a more lengthy stride, the sign of a tall horse.

A full blood could have read more. Twine was an average tracker, less gifted than a full blood would have been, but for as long as he tracked the sign was clear enough until the outlaw veered northward, entered the water of a busy little creek and there, because the water was no longer roiled he had to guess whether the highwayman had gone north or south.

He guessed wrong; if the outlaw had ridden south he would have come to the settlement. Twine paralleled the creek northward until close to sundown then turned back toward Jefferson.

Not unexpectedly, by the time Twine had eaten, cared for his mount and fired up the lamp in the jail-house, Cal Lott came in, listened to what Twine said and, with fire in his belly, told the constable if the hold-up had occurred in that place called Point of Rocks it wouldn't be a coincidence; most of the earlier hold-ups had occurred there and as far as Cal Lott was concerned the person who had taken his moneybox up yonder would as certain as grass was green be one of the same earlier highwaymen who had stopped stages at that same spot.

Twine did not disagree. His only remark, given drily, was that if it was one of the earlier highwaymen he'd be older than most highwaymen were. Cal Lott threw up his hands.

'Age's got nothin' to do with it,

Twine. I'll tell you what I know from years back; they had a hideout somewhere in the northerly mountains, most likely far up there. Years back, I was up there bear huntin'; there's prehistoric caves and whatnot where a man could never get caught because from up that high you can see southward all the way to the settlement.'

Twine had patience. He heard the storekeeper out, closed the roadway door after him, returned to his desk and felt in a lower drawer for a bottle of whiskey he kept there, as he'd said often, for snake bites.

The Jefferson countryside had snakes, but no one had ever encountered one in the jailhouse or other inhabited places.

The following morning Twine was in the saddle before sunrise and reached the robbery site with dawn breaking. He picked up the trail again and this time, with an entire day ahead of him, he paralleled the creek until he found where a rider had come out of the water leaving clear sign of a shod animal with a long stride, and didn't stop again for better than two hours, not until he was close enough to the cliff front to make out the hawk-like face high above.

Here, where prehistoric rocks lay scattered, some as large as a horse, there were elk picking grass among the rocks, paying no attention to a saddle horse grazing among them.

Twine got into cover where two huge rocks lay side by side, dismounted, looped his reins around a low branch of a puny fir tree and eased between the two-storey rocks to study the area. That horse among the elk had dry sweat marks where a saddle had been.

Twine eased his right hand down to tug loose the thong over his six-gun and examined squares of the area individually before blocking in the next square. He was looking for a camp. At the eastern-most edge of the boulder field what he saw held him motionless. Clearly, the cabin was old. It had green moss atop a sagging roof. It also had a propped-up pole corral with a paint horse dozing in sunlight.

Two horses meant two people. The paint horse weighed about 900 pounds and was short coupled. The bay horse with the grazing elk was about sixteen hands tall with the skimpy mane and tail of a thoroughbred, or perhaps half thoroughbred. He was built for speed and with a long back he would have a long stride.

Twine completed his deductions and was satisfied Cal Lott's moneybox would be inside the cabin when a deep voice using words spaced well apart said, 'Drop the gun!'

Twine froze. Whoever he was his voice and words were unmistakably serious. Twine emptied his holster and would have turned, but that same voice stopped that. 'Don't move!'

Twine didn't; he'd heard deadly serious men before. This one sounded not only serious but professionally calm. His next order was, 'Walk ahead of me to the house. Don't do anythin' foolish.'

Twine had to squeeze between the big rocks, the man behind him seemed not to have that trouble which told Twine that whoever the man was he wasn't thick.

Someone years back, probably the builder of the log house, had cleared the rocks, had made a stone fence with them so that the hike to the house was over rock-free graze.

Something Twine hadn't noticed before was the thin spindrift of smoke arising into the still air from a crudely fashioned but evidently serviceable rock chimney.

When they were within spitting distance of the door, the calm-voiced man said, 'Hold it.'

Twine stopped. Up until now he hadn't spoken, now he did. 'Mister, I'm the law. I got no idea who you are, but I followed your sign to this place after the Jefferson stage was robbed.'

The calm voice answered without

haste or noticeable concern. 'I know who you are, the constable from Jefferson. Mr Fourch, you'd've done better to lose the sign like you done yesterday. Have you got a boot knife or a derringer?'

'No, don't have either.'

'Open the door an' go inside. Stop when you're beyond the door. Mind your manners, Mr Fourch.'

Twine didn't need the admonition. He opened the door, stepped inside and was immediately struck by two things: it was unnecessarily hot inside and it smelled of something that could have been disinfectant.

The cabin had no window. It was gloomy, day and night. Twine waited for his eyes to adjust and the man behind him kicked the door closed, lighted a candle and said, 'Go sit on the bench. Keep your hands in your lap.'

Twine did as ordered. The bench had one short leg. He adjusted to that.

There were two bunks on opposite sides of the room. The fire in its mud-wattled stone area gave what little light was available and that was of a flickering variety.

The man with the gun said, 'Turn around, Mr Fourch.'

Twine obeyed and stopped breathing for three seconds. The man he was facing was familiar. His name was Justin Abbot; he was the stage company's Jefferson corralyard boss. He holstered his handgun, slouched against the door as he spoke. 'I wish to hell you'd gone manhunting in some other direction.' He shrugged, crossed to a bed built against the west wall and spoke again while looking down. 'You put me in a fix, Mr Fourch. No one else came along, mostly I expect because it's a long, uncomfortable ride.'

Justin Abbot turned. 'Come over here. Stop at the foot of the bed.'

Again Twine obeyed. The candle didn't brighten the room very much, but the fireplace did. Twine stood at the foot of the bed, speechless. Under a pile of moth-eaten old blankets was a woman whose age was made indistinguishable because of her wrinkled and contorted face. She was unmistakeably a full blood.

Justin Abbot said, 'I got no idea what it is, but she's had it some time, whatever it is.'

'You found her up here?' Twine asked, and the corralyard boss shook his head.

'I was elk hunting some time back, about a week. I found her soaked from rain, feverish and curled into a ball in a little clearing with a spotted horse.' Abbot paused regarding the woman whose jet-black eyes didn't leave his face.

'I don't know anythin' about doctorin' or sickness. She told me it's a bad spirit livin' in her. She inherited it from her father. He scalped the bugle boy with Custer some years back. The bad spirit was in him too. It eventually killed him.' Another pause. 'She said when he died all his hair fell out.'

Twine raised his eyes. 'You'll be goin' back with me for robbin' the stage.' He looked down briefly. 'I expect we can rig somethin' to take her back on.'

Abbot shook his head. 'She'd never live through the trip.' He looked steadily at Twine Fourch. 'I didn't rob that coach. She did. Yonder's the money-box.'

Twine looked around, saw the box and looked back. 'You said she'd been sick a long time.'

'She has.'

'How does a sick old squaw rob a stage?'

'She took my horse, went down there, robbed the coach and rode back. I found her lyin' unconscious in the mud with a moneybox.'

Twine returned to the bench, sat down and gazed into the fireplace.

2

A Return of a Ghost

His intention had to do with using the blanket roll tied aft on his cantle, and head back the following day. He wasn't hungry, although he should have been, but when the corralyard boss put a dented tin plate of stew before him at the only other bit of furniture, an ancient, battered table, he ate.

Later, after Justin Abbot had got broth down the woman and had stoked up the fire, he jerked his head and Twine followed him out into a star-speckled, clear cool night. Abbot forked hay to the spotted horse, leaned on the rickety old corral and looked at the eating animal as he spoke.

'She's bad off.'

Twine did not have to be told that. 'How did she take your horse without you knowin' it, an' how did she manage to carry that moneybox all the way up here?'

Abbot shook his head. 'I don't know. She also took my boots.' He faced Twine Fourch. 'Sick as she is it's not how she done those things, but why.'

'What did she say?'

'Nothin'; I think she understands English, but she don't talk.' Abbot's gaze slid past to the cabin where a feeble candle burned. 'I come up here hunting. I can't stay away from the corralyard, there's things to be done, schedules to be minded . . . would you stay with her so's I can go back?'

The question shocked Twine Fourch. 'I got a job down yonder. I can't just up and . . . '

'Maybe she'll talk to you. In'ian to In'ian.'

'What kind of In'ian is she? There's different languages, an' I don't remember very much anyway.'

'She's dying.'

Again, Twine did not need to be

told that. 'In'ians die like everyone else,' he said.

'Constable, she's old an' sick. It don't matter what she is, does it? Keep the fire goin'. It's too hot for me, but she starts shakin' if the fire goes out. For Chris' sake she's a human bein'.'

'She's a full blood In'ian.'

That shocked the corralyard boss. He stared at Twine Fourch. 'That makes a difference? She can't take care of herself, she's got to be fed. She used up whatever strength she had goin' down yonder, stoppin' that coach an' ridin' back.'

Twine watched the spotted horse eat and sounded almost dispassionate when he said, 'Why? Why'd she do it, her sick an' dyin', why do all that horse-backing and take the moneybox?'

Abbot gave a frank answer. 'I got no idea. I asked her an' all she did was look up at me. Constable, when someone's dyin' they'd have a reason, wouldn't they? She damned near didn't

21

make it. Except for me comin' along, her lyin' all night in the rain, shakin' bad an' unconscious . . . We owe it to her to keep her warm'n fed even though she's In'ian. They got feelings like we have. I don't understand any of it except that dyin' folks should be made easy. It don't matter, In'ian or not.'

Twine straightened up off the corral. 'You got some whiskey?' he asked, and Abbot shook his head.

'I dribbled the last of it down her yesterday. Stay here, look after her'n I'll be back as quick as I can an' bring some whiskey.'

Twine turned to regard the old log house. He said, 'I can't just up an' stay here. My job's to mind things at the settlement.' He paused. From the direction of the cabin came a trilling sound. Twine said, 'Death chant,' and faced the corralyard boss. 'All right, but you return no later'n day after tomorrow, otherwise I leave and head back.' He turned to consider the paint horse. 'Looks in good shape. Where did she come from?'

Justin Abbot made a humourless grunt of laughter. 'Maybe you can get some answers, I never got any.'

'The way she looked an' listened I'd say she likely hears an' understands. Head back before sunrise. I'll be waiting. How did you know I was hidin' in those rocks?'

'The paint horse told me. He stared, wouldn't eat, just stared. It could've been a cougar or a bear. I scouted you up by listening. I'll be back quick as I can.'

'Day after tomorrow, an' I don't think it'd be a good idea to say anything.'

Abbot nodded and left Twine at the corral, went to the house and stoked up the fire. It had kept him busy the last few days finding fireplace-length dry wood.

He sat on the edge of the old woman's bed and told her he had to leave but would return, that the

23

big 'breed lawman would stay in his place. He took a shrivelled, claw-like hand, held it briefly then went after his riding gear. She watched his every move.

He and Twine Fourch met at the door. Twine said, 'Fetch back some laudanum from Cal Lott's store.'

It was one of the interesting things about time that its passage, slow as it seemed to pass, was surprisingly swift when people existed in a vacuum of crisis.

Twine should have slept well. He didn't, not through any fault of the old squaw, she rarely made a sound; she was adept at stifling sounds of pain.

It was something Twine felt but could not define. It was restlessness and some small, inner sensation of helplessness. Rarely in his life had he been helpless, but, as he sat on the edge of the old woman's bunk spooning meat broth to her, he felt physically oversized and capably inadequate. He tried some of the few Shoshoni words he remembered and was rewarded with an unwavering black-eyed gaze accompanied by no sound. He didn't believe the woman was Shoshoni, maybe Crow or Dakota, maybe Assiniboine or Lakota. He knew none of those languages. He inadvertently did something that brought a faint but unmistakable expression to her face. He put a large hand atop a shrivelled claw and smiled. She didn't smile back, but something passed between them. He stoked up the fire. It was too hot for him so he went out where dawn was breaking, heard two owls call, one from the timber to the east, the second owl answering from the west.

Stars were fading, the air was chilly. He went back inside. The old woman was asleep. He hefted the stolen moneybox, wondered how she had gotten it this far, upended it and sat on it. Her eyes opened. She looked steadily at him without blinking and held up one hand using *wibluto*.

He got her a tin cup of water from a bucket, held it for her as she drank, wiped her mouth and chin and would have arisen from the cot. She made a feeble gesture, brushed the back of one of his hands and formed sound with her mouth with no sound coming.

He went out to the corral to fork loose grass hay to the spotted horse and noticed something he hadn't seen before, a single braid on the mane on the right side behind the ear. If there had ever been a piece of coloured cloth, perhaps a feather in the braid, they were gone.

Braids had significance, but only providing something significant was braided into the hair.

He went back inside. The old woman watched everything he did until he cooked up a fresh batch of broth, then she got that strange, faint, gentle look again. While he was feeding her, the spotted horse nickered. Twine started to arise. As before, she brushed his hand with her hand and this time when she worked her lips with obvious effort the sound was some kind of either a pleading or a warning. He patted her hand, arose and went to the door. It was violently kicked inward.

The man standing there was not as dark as Twine, but his features were unmistakably Indian. He held his pistol low and cocked it. 'Back up,' he said. 'Keep your hands in front. Sit on the bench.'

The stranger shoved his cocked gun against Twine's chest as he leaned to disarm the Jefferson township lawman. He moved out of reach, looked in the direction of the squaw's bed and back as he said something in a language Twine didn't remember hearing before. From the bed, the old woman spoke barely audible words in the same language. The 'breed with the gun darted a swift look in the direction of the moneybox, faced Twine again and seemed to loosen a little.

'Take off the badge,' he said and Twine obeyed. As the other man took the badge, he spat on it and flung it toward the fireplace. It did not land in the fire.

Twine said, 'Do you know the old woman?'

The answer was crisp and harsh. 'I know her. So should you. You should know me too except that we never knew each other after soldiers came. My name is Hauck Fourshay. I know your name. I wish the other one had stayed and you had gone back.'

Twine twisted to look in the direction of the cot. The old woman was crying without making a sound. Twine looked back at the Indian-looking paleskin.

The man sneered. 'Do you know what she did? She escaped from Fort Sedgewich the night before the others were loaded into cattle cars for the ride to a reservation. She stole horses, walked and crawled when she couldn't no longer walk. It took her half a year. She stole me back from the whiteskin preacher. We lived in a cave under the stone-face beak. Do you know my

28

name, not your name, but the Crow name?'

Twine shook his head.

'It is Lost One. My name would be Joe Stiles. That was the God-man's Christian name. He was a fair man but I was a 'breed In'ian. I think he was happy when she stole me out of my bed in the night.' The uncompromisingly hostile look was in place when the 'breed spoke again.

'She said I could make a good way in the whiteman's world. She was gone one morning. I tracked her, saw her stop the stage and ride away with the moneybox. I lost her sign when it rained, but I knew the painted horse. I found it.'

The 'breed leathered his handgun and looked in the direction of his mother. 'She told me about you, how you'd found a place in the white-man's world. She took that moneybox so's I could buy my way into the white-man's world.' The sneer returned. 'Money is the blood and soul of white people.

29

You know that, don't you?'

Twine arose, went to the cot and sat on the side of it, he took one bony hand and held it. 'He is my brother?'

The old woman jutted her jaw, the Indian sign for the word yes.

He dug for his big bandanna, wiped her face and put the bandanna in her hand. She squeezed it.

Behind him, the unfriendly man spoke. 'Is there a whiteskin medicine man in Jefferson?'

Twine shook his head.

'Then I will find one and bring him here.'

This time Twine shook his head, he said, 'Don't do anythin' that'll rouse up folks. There'll be a reward an' that'll bring bounty men.' Twine arose. 'Come outside with me.' He closed the door after them and spoke bluntly. 'She needs peace. Whatever it is it'll kill her. You stir up manhunters an' they'll drag her somewhere to be tried for what she done. That would kill her.'

Stiles said, 'She deserves better'n to

die in an old shack.'

'I don't think it matters where a person dies. It matters how they die. Leave her here. Don't stir folks up. They're stirred up enough.'

'I could carry her to the cave. It's been our home a long time. She has an old tintype of my father an' the prayer feathers of my grandmother.'

'Go get them, bring them here. Listen to me, she is goin' to die. I want her to die at peace, warm, fed and looked after.'

The sneer returned as the other 'breed said, 'What you want for her. Do you know why she cried? She knew who your mother was an' you didn't know. You belong to the other people.'

Twine's temper was rising. 'Get her special things an' bring them back.'

'An' what about the whiteskin who brought her here? He'd shoot me on sight.'

'No he won't. Why did he bother bringin' an old sick In'ian here? He didn't have to, an old woman lyin' in the mud.'

'Tell me why he did it?'

Twine's answer was short. 'Ask him. He'll be back tomorrow with medicine.'

'You are sure?'

'His word is good.'

The sneer resurfaced. 'Is there such a white man? He'll return with a posse.'

Twine's retort was short and angry. 'You damned misfit. For two bits I'd . . . '

The gun appeared in a steady hand. For a long moment Joe Stiles looked steadily at Twine Fourch, then relaxed, holstered the weapon and walked in the direction of some distant trees.

When Twine returned to the house the fire was dying. He fed it until it blazed then went to sit on the edge of the old woman's bed. She tried to use the bandanna to hide her face, but the tears flowed. He leaned and did something he hadn't done more than once or twice in his life. He kissed her cheek which didn't lessen the tears, it increased them.

He went outside to feed the spotted horse. The hay was old with abundant spider webs and mouse droppings. His horse wouldn't have touched it. The paint horse had no scruples. He'd missed a lot of meals.

There had been another boy child and another child, a tiny girl who had died while her people were waiting for the cattle cars.

When he returned he stoked up the fire, sat on the edge of the old woman's bed expressionless and silent. She put a wrinkled, bony hand atop one of his hands. He avoided the unwavering steady gaze. Later when he went back outside there was no sign of his brother. The absence didn't bother him. There were abiding ancient instincts which the white-man's world couldn't extinguish.

That night was the first he slept through without troublesome thoughts and in the morning because the fire was down to coals he went out back to search for wood. Because this had been done before he had to extend his search a considerable distance up into the timber. There, he loaded up with deadfalls and started back. As always the passage of time was only significant if there was light. He had been gone most of the morning.

There was a hobbled horse eating its head off. Twine dumped some of his dry wood and went to the cabin. Because he had recognized the horse he knew who would be inside and he was right. The corralyard boss had his back to the door arranging groceries on shelves and turned only when Twine walked in, dropped wood near the fireplace and said, 'You get the laudanum?'

Instead of replying, Justin Abbot jerked his head and continued to fill the shelves.

Twine went to the cot. The old woman was sleeping, her breathing was deep and evenly spaced.

34

Abbot finally spoke. 'Who was the visitor?'

'Her son.'

Justin paused at his arranging, faced around and said, 'I had to lie like a trooper. Folks down yonder got worked up when you didn't come back. They figured you found the highwayman an' he killed you. Cal Lott's runnin' around like a chicken with its head chopped off. Him an' old man Severn went to make up a posse to find your body.'

Twine was less surprised than worried. Bean Severn had been an army scout; he could track a fly across a glass window. His thoughts were scattered when the corralyard boss spoke again.

'Her son . . . ?'

Twine told Justin Abbot the entire story and the corralyard boss stared at him. 'She's your ma?'

Twine nodded.

'An' this bronco of hers is your brother?'

Again Twine nodded.

35

'Are there any more?'

'A sister. She died years back. I thought he had died too.'

The blazing fire drove Abbot further from it. He paused at the old woman's bed looking down. 'I gave her a light dose of the laudanum. She smiled. I knew it works fast but not that fast.'

'How much did you bring?'

Instead of answering the question, Justin Abbot said, 'Cal looked at me real funny when I asked for it. Twine, like him or not he's not a fool.'

Abbot sat at the ancient table looking up. 'Where is the bronco?'

'I don't know. He upped and left the way they do. He'll be back.'

'Is he a hostile?'

'Well, some missionary folks raised him. He wasn't here long.'

'How did he find her?'

'That spotted horse out there was his. He tracked her.' Twine stood beside the bed looking down. When he spoke his voice was inflectionless, the way a voice is when its owner isn't thinking of conversation. 'He wasn't friendly, but he'd have his reasons. He's like the others I've known; to them I got an In'ian outside an' a white man inside. They don't trust men like me.'

He finally went to the rickety bench. 'Cal's goin' to make a manhunt? Justin, old Bean Severn'll pick up the sign sure as I'm settin' here.'

Abbot had arrived at that conclusion before leaving Jefferson to return. He said, 'How well do you know the old rascal?'

'As well as I want to. I've had to lock him up a dozen times, for stealin' chickens, being drunk and mean, for leerin' at womenfolk.'

'I got a notion, Twine. I'll ride back down, catch the old bastard scoutin' ahead, offer him twenty dollars to lead Cal away from up here.'

Twine slowly inclined his head. It could work; Bean Severn would sell his mother for a handful of silver. 'Let your horse rest then start back.

Be careful the others don't see you.'

'How about the bronco?'

'You'll be gone before he can get back. All the same, watch your back.'

'Can you handle him?'

Twine answered belatedly because the old woman made a soft sigh, but he nodded. 'I can handle him. How long ago did you give her the medicine?'

'Hour, maybe two hours. Not much, she's skinny as a snake. With her don't take but a tad.'

3

A Meeting

Twine found the whiskey Abbot had brought and took it outside with him. The day was dying, spirals of a descending sun showed where daylight found openings among the forest giants.

The air was fragrant as it usually was after warm days made tree sap run. He sipped the whiskey. All he remembered of his father was of a large, blustery, bearded man with twinkling dark eyes and a powerful accent. His memory of the dying old woman in the cabin was of a quiet person who dug roots, gathered wood, made things from animal skins and occasionally cried in her bed robes. He knew nothing of her past. Between the time he had been taken from her and this dying day he knew nothing.

He didn't have to know. She had been among those making The Trail of Tears. Everyone knew about that. Her hands told a lot. He took another swallow of whiskey and wondered about a fate that had brought him up under the beak of Stone Mountain to find she had lived through, and more, what his brother had told him. For a moment he loathed the blustery bearded man with the twinkling eyes before he took another swallow and returned to the cabin to spoon food into the old woman.

The laudanum had worn off. She was doubled into a knot of pain. He tossed two scantlings into the fire, rummaged until he found the little blue bottle, and forced her mouth open with the spoon.

While he waited he made broth of stringy jerky. He had returned to the house hungry. Afterwards he had no appetite.

He wasn't curious about what was killing her; he was fatalistic; that was the other part of his heritage. When the time came . . .

The paint horse nickered.

Twine remained with the old woman as gradually she came out of her knot. He saw the relaxation arrive slowly and smiled at her.

She parted her lips, but the sound was harsh and indistinguishable and that frustrated her. She tried harder. He brushed her cheek gently and arose. She had expressive black eyes; they followed him to the door.

Two men were outside, one was Justin Abbot, the one behind Abbot was Joe Stiles with an uncocked old six-gun in his fist.

Abbot said, 'Nice evenin' isn't it?'

The 'breed guided Abbot inside with his six-gun barrel. His gaze flicked toward the cot then back as he told the corralyard boss to sit on the bench, which Abbot did, gazing dispassionately at Twine who faced the other 'breed but addressed Justin Abbot.

'How far did you get?'

'Mile or two. I didn't see him but I felt him. I dismounted to look back an' there he was.'

Stiles spoke in short sentences. 'He was goin' back. He'd bring others.'

In exasperation, Twine replied irritably, 'You damn fool, there's riders comin'. He was goin' down to buy off their sign reader.'

Stiles answered defensively. 'He didn't say that.'

'You wouldn't have believed him.' Twine stood a moment regarding the 'breed with lighter skin. 'Did you bring her things?'

'Tied in a sack on my horse.'

'Go get them.'

Stiles didn't move. He and Twine looked steadily at one another until Twine spoke again. 'Put up that damned gun an' fetch the sack. *Go!*'

Stiles left the house and Justin slumped. 'They'll be gettin' close,' he said. 'Come mornin' they'll be here.'

'Go find 'em, Justin. If you can't

catch old Severn apart run off their horses.'

Abbot arose from the bench, glanced briefly in the direction of the cot, reset his hat and mumbled something as he left the cabin.

Twine retrieved his badge, rubbed it a couple of times on his trouser leg before pinning it in place.

Joe Stiles returned, stopped stone still and asked where his captive was. Twine explained. Joe Stiles put down the little sack, went outside and closed the door after him.

Twine took the sack to the bedside, emptied its scanty contents, picked out a nearly illegible tintype photograph of a bushy-faced, smiling, large man and handed it to the old woman. She cried.

He went outside. Descending night was still and quiet. When the pinto horse saw him it nickered. He told the animal it had had all the feed it was going to get until morning and walked a short distance southward to listen.

The silence was deep and enduring.

He walked back, stood a while outside then entered, lighted two candles, stoked up the fire and sat on the edge of the old woman's cot. She tried to tell him something which he could not understand. She put a claw of a hand to her throat and tried again, this time with considerable effort.

He nodded, wiped a drying tear from her face and told her that Joe Stiles, or whatever his name was, had left. He made an incorrect assumption. This time her son would most likely not return.

She raised an arm that was wasted flesh around bone. He looked in the right direction. She tried one more time to speak, failed and in a combination of exasperation and exhaustion let the arm drop.

Twine went in the direction she had pointed, hefted the moneybox with its metal corners, large hasp and steel padlock, put it atop the table. It was heavy, they were made of steel-reinforced oak; they had weight even when they were empty.

This box was scarred; it had been used a long time. He considered shooting off the lock but didn't; a gunshot would upset the hell out of the old woman. He knew what was inside it, not how much, probably Cal Lott would be the only one to know that.

The old woman had her jaws clamped tight. She had beads of sweat. The pain had returned. She would have died before asking for relief.

He got the blue bottle, the dented old spoon and ladled the laudanum. It required no more than ten minutes for her jaws to loosen, for her expressive black eyes to mirror gratitude.

He sat down again. She covered one of his large, powerful hands with five fingers that were bony, cold and gentle.

He told her all he remembered of his childhood. He also told her he had believed for years she and the children had perished either on their way to the reservation or after they got there.

The longer he talked the more drowsy she became until she finally slept. He put the claw of a hand under the covers, kissed her cheek and went outside with the whiskey bottle. It helped, but only time could resolve the lump in his throat and the ache in his heart.

He had no idea of the time when he heard the very faint echo of a gunshot. He was tempted to rig out and ride southward except that he had no idea how long he might be gone before the laudanum wore off. The old woman was getting near the end. He would not allow her to die in agony or alone.

He made no attempt to analyse his feelings; he hadn't seen her since he had been a child, had believed her dead. What he felt had little to do with a possible relationship. It was impossible not to look at her and not know genuine heartache. As Justin had said, tomahawk or not she was a human being.

His solemn moment passed when a shod hoof struck stone. He could not see the rider, but he sensed his direction and moved soundlessly to the shelter of a ragged old fir tree which was near the end of the trail. Its core was rotten.

It wasn't one rider, it was two, one leading the horse of the other rider who rode slumped with a death grip on the saddle horn.

When Twine stepped in weak moonlight, the first horseman yanked to a stop, squinted and said, 'Your gawddamned bronco liked to got us both killed. I thought they was like ghosts.'

'Is he hurt, Justin?'

'Yes, the silly son of a bitch is hurt. I had Bean Severn away from the others, offered him twenty dollars when this idiot let go a warwhoop and jumped Severn from behind me. The old man got off a shot before I kicked his arm. Your In'ian was sittin' on the ground like a sick bear. I didn't see the others but that shot roused 'em swearin' an' runnin' around after their horses.

'I got this idiot on his horse and come back as fast as I could. Move aside, we'll unload him at the cabin.'

As Joe Stiles' horse plodded past Twine saw the look on the rider's face.

They got him down in front of the house. Justin said, 'Take him inside. I got to look after the horses.'

When Twine opened the door carrying the old woman's son she struggled to sit up, couldn't do it and fell back making harsh sounds.

By candlelight Twine put his brother atop the old table, held one of the candles close and swore under his breath. Fortunately for Joe Stiles, old Severn's shot had been wild. The slug had missed dead centre by about ten or twelve inches, instead of the brisket the bullet had shattered the 'breed's upper arm on the left side. He had bled hard and was still bleeding when Twine got the second candle, cut away cloth and used a sleeve to tie off the bleeding.

Joe Stiles wavered between consciousness and unconsciousness. It didn't help that in the poor light the old woman was croaking a death chant.

He went to the cot, showed with his hand where her son had been injured and patted a bony shoulder. 'He'll be all right. It'll take time but he won't die.'

The old woman's tears did not diminish. To her, whose lifetime had been fear, ostracism and anguish, this was another 'burden' among many.

Justin Abbot's disgust showed in everything he did and said, 'The damned fool, just when Severn had agreed and taken the money this idiot comes charging out of the night. Twine, sure as we're standing here Severn'll bring them here.'

Abbot went to the cooking area for a cup of coffee. The old woman's stifled groans irritated him. He turned, cup in hand and glared.

The wound was the kind that looked worse than it was, but blood was everywhere. Twine leaned and softly spoke. Joe Stiles looked at him from unreadable black eyes. 'He was telling that old man where you are.'

Twine slowly shook his head. 'He was paying the old man to lead the riders away from here.'

The black eyes didn't waver.

From over by the fire, visible but barely so, Justin Abbot said, 'You damned fool', and flung the coffee into the fire. He didn't speak again, he went outside to look after the animals. He was as angry as he had ever been. While he was out there a night bird called, the sound was not very different from the cry of a kitten.

When he returned to the cabin the old woman was asleep, her breathing was steady. Twine had given her laudanum.

Joe Stiles was no longer atop the table, he was sitting at it, one arm hanging, the other arm raised to support his face. He wouldn't look at Abbot.

Justin told Twine they had to leave this place and he cast a glance toward the old woman on her cot, wagged his head, made a motion for Twine to follow, and returned to the chilly night. Out there he said, 'How do we move her? She's skin an' bones, can't hardly even hold her head up. An' take her where?'

Twine had no answers except to say, 'They'll be comin' with first light.'

'Let 'em come. You'n I've done the best we can. When they get here they aren't going to be friendly toward us, but I got a clear conscience.'

'We'll give 'em the damned money-box.'

Abbot shook his head. 'That won't placate 'em. Not now. You'n I'll be lucky if they don't lynch us. Sure as hell's hot they'll hang the idiot inside.'

The door behind them opened, weak and unsteady light backgrounded Joe Stiles. He held to the door, looked out at them and said, 'I can cover the tracks. We can go up yonder to the cave.'

Justin regarded the injured man stonily. 'Mister, they got the best sign reader in the country. Nobody can hide tracks from Bean Severn.'

Somewhere southward a horse blew its nose. All three men became momentarily rigid. Twine said, 'He's leadin' 'em', and headed back to the house.

Justin did the same thing. At the door, the man whose clothing had drying blood said, 'How was I to know?'

Justin brushed roughly past without a sound.

Twine was standing beside the cot looking down. Without looking around he told the old woman's other son to explain to her in their language what had to be done, and without delay.

Stiles came closer as he addressed his mother. She said something which made Joe Stiles to reply curtly. He

52

looked at Twine. 'You understand any of that?' he asked.

Twine shook his head.

'She said to leave her here. They wanted the stage robber. You'n me an' your friend didn't do nothin' but help her. She said give 'em the moneybox, get ahorseback an' leave while we can.'

Twine considered the old woman. As long as they'd been together she hadn't been able to say ten words. He looked at his brother. 'You made that up.'

Stiles gave look for look. 'Some of it. She's right, leave her here. We can't move her anyway. She couldn't stand goin' back to the cave.'

Twine crossed to the moneybox, picked it up, kicked the door open and walked out into the night. Behind him Justin said, 'It won't work. They'll take the box an' still come here.'

Joe Stiles had to sit down, he was weak. From the bench, he considered the open door where cold air was coming in. He changed the direction of his gaze only when Justin said, 'If

Cal Lott is with 'em he'll . . . '

'Who is Cal Lott?'

Justin pointed. 'His money's in that box. Maybe he won't let 'em hang me or Twine, but sure as hell he'll hang you.'

The 'breed arose, by wavering, puny candlelight he looked like some kind of other-worldly demon. 'You carry her an' I'll show you the way.'

Justin's gaze was sardonic. 'An' what about your brother?'

Joe Stiles had to sit down again. 'While he's stallin' them we can get clear of this place. They'll never track us in the dark.'

Justin repeated it. 'What about your brother?'

'He's the law; he's got the moneybox.'

Justin shook his head. 'I don't leave him. I don't know who they are, but you can bet sound money after that gunshot they'll be loaded for bear.'

'I'll carry her up there. You can stay here.'

Justin snorted. 'Mister, you couldn't

carry her a hunnert feet.'

Twine returned without the money-box. He opened the door slowly enough to attract the attention of the three people inside and hesitated in the doorway, expressionless and unarmed.

He was given a punch from behind and entered the room.

Behind him were three men with pistols in their hands. Justin knew them. He sank down on the bench. The man directly behind Twine was large, burly and balding Calvin Lott from the Jefferson general store. His left arm was folded around the moneybox.

Behind him was a rangeman named Bailey, Jess Bailey, who rode for a cow outfit south of Jefferson. Bailey was not an impressive individual, he was about average in height, thin, unshaven with grey eyes and a bear-trap mouth. The last man to come inside was Bean Severn. He had age on him, was weathered brown and wrinkled with pale eyes.

The bullying, short-tempered store-keeper spoke first. 'All right, Constable. Now we got the pair of you . . . who's the 'breed?'

Severn interrupted. 'He's the feller tried to kill me.' Severn eyed Joe Stiles. 'I thought I'd killed you.'

Twine's brother spoke coldly. 'Nobody can shoot straight in the dark.'

The newcomers looked toward the cot and Bean Severn said, 'Who's she?'

Twine didn't answer, Joe Stiles did. 'My mother. She's sick.'

The old frontierman leathered his weapon, went to the bedside and squinted hard. The light was poor. He leaned and said something guttural. The old woman looked steadily at him without making a sound, but she moved slightly under the blankets and Bean Severn reached, flung back the blankets and held the bone and sinew of her right hand. With his other hand he pried the under-and-over .44 calibre derringer from her fingers.

Twine stared.

Severn dropped the small pistol, yanked the covers back into place and smiled wolfishly. The old woman's black gaze did not leave his face. Severn spoke again in that guttural language and the old woman expectorated on him.

Instead of lashing out, the old man laughed, straightened up, faced the others and said, 'Red Moon's woman,' and added more as the others neither moved nor spoke. 'Red Moon was the Crow name for her man. His real name was Fourshay. I met him a couple of times years back. In'ians called him Red Moon. He was one of them French Canadian trappers. Big, fat man.'

Severn turned back slowly toward the cot. 'No good son of a bitch, wasn't he?'

The old woman's eyes never left Severn, but Joe Stiles started toward the cot. The bull-necked storekeeper caught him by his right arm and spun him away. Lott released his grip, raised his six-gun, cocked it and pointed it at Stiles's face from a distance of no more than eight or ten feet.

Twine spoke sharply. 'Put that gun down, Cal.'

The fierce-tempered storekeeper swung the gun in Twine's direction. 'Never trust a 'breed,' he said. 'You knew about that robbery; how much of a cut was you to get?'

The lean rangeman was holstering his six-gun when he spoke without raising his voice. 'Leave it be, Mister Lott. He's unarmed.'

'Damned, stealin', lyin' 'breed,' Lott said, glaring. 'I figured when you was gone so long you was part of it. Take off that badge!'

4

A Killing

Twine made no move to remove the badge and Cal Lott exploded; he cursed Twine and lunged to yank the badge off. For a heavy man he was fast. He had Twine's shirt before anyone reacted.

When Lott wrenched the badge it came away with part of Twine's shirt.

Twine moved, both arms rising. The rangeman named Bailey would have moved to interfere, but Justin Abbot caught him low, by the shellbelt, and flung him sideways. Bailey didn't fall but he would have except for the wall.

Lott came in like a bull, head lowered, ham-sized fists cocked. Twine did not give ground, which was a mistake. When Lott's weight hit him Twine had to step back and aim a fist.

Lott gave him no chance. He swung without a target, but as close as they were he had to connect and he did.

Twine sagged and Justin started forward. This time the rangeman yanked so hard Justin fell, hitting his head on the side of the bed, and crumpled in a ball on the floor. Before he could arise, Cal Lott's fury and weight had Twine Fourch wobbling from side to side to miss blows, but not very well.

The old woman croaked something that Stiles understood. He was reaching for his holster when the rangeman collared him too, struck his gun wrist with a six-gun barrel and growled for him to stay out of it.

While this was happening, Twine landed a lucky blow. It staggered the heavy man who back-pedalled as he recovered.

Twine's blunder was that he did not follow up. His side hurt and where he'd been stopped by a rock-hard fist with his stomach, he felt sick.

Lott stood back shaking his head, then charged. This time Twine waited until the last moment before stepping sideways.

As Lott went past, pawing at air, Twine balanced on his toes and hit the heavier man under the right ear.

Lott didn't fall, he collapsed. His knees sprung, his massive torso sagged and he went down as slowly as a log.

The rangeman wig-wagged with his six-gun, meaning Twine was not to put the boots to the fallen man. Twine ignored the warning, braced with one hand atop the table and sucked air.

The old woman dropped back. Stiles said something and for the first time in days she smiled.

Jess Bailey put up his six-gun, considered the large, balding man lying as though dead or asleep and said, 'Damned fool.'

There were no other comments. Twine needed fresh air and went just beyond the doorway to get it. Bean Severn, who'd stayed well clear during the fight, came up behind him and said, 'You can have the twenty dollars back.'

Twine looked around. 'Keep it. Buy yourself a week-long drunk, but don't do it in town. Did Cal hire you?'

'Yes. Me'n the cowboy. He was in town for some mail. They'll wonder what happened to him. Him an' another feller. The other feller stayed back. We didn't need him anyway.'

Cal Lott was recovering, slowly and ponderously, but he was recovering. No one helped him arise. He used the bench and the edge of the table for that.

Jess Bailey found the whiskey and poured two fingers' worth into a tin cup and handed it to the storekeeper, whose gaze was fixed on the dark man just beyond the door.

The rangeman also went outside. He wagged his head at Twine. 'I wouldn't have bet on you,' he said, and mingled with the darkness as he went in the direction of the grassy place where he'd left his hobbled horse.

Twine was turning to re-enter the cabin when he thought he heard voices. He only hesitated, it was common for men to talk to their horses, particularly rangemen who went days on end with no other company.

The old woman watched Twine with sparkling eyes and enunciated with difficulty when she said something he did not understand. He smiled, leaned to pat her face and went to mix some laudanum. It was said laudanum was not only an effective pain killer but was also a powerful narcotic. Maybe it was, but the old woman suffered the agonies of hell without it.

He spoonfed her and she swallowed without taking her eyes off his face.

Joe Stiles appeared at the bedside. The old woman croaked again and Stiles addressed Twine. 'She said you have much in you of your father. You don't give up.'

Twine smiled crookedly. His stomach hurt as did his ribs. He took Stiles aside.

'She'll die when we leave her.'

Stiles gave a pragmatic answer. 'She's not here for long anyway.'

Twine shook his head. 'I'm not going to leave her.'

To that his brother with the lighter complexion said, 'You got no choice.'

Twine removed the badge from his torn shirt, tossed it atop the table and went over to where Cal Lott was sitting hunched. He sat down beside the storekeeper and said, 'You got your moneybox.'

Lott turned. 'That badge . . . '

'It's on the table. You can take it with you.'

Lott's face creased into a scowl. 'Because of her, for Chris'sake? Look at her, she won't last another few days.'

Twine could have explained, but he didn't; instead he said, 'You come for the moneybox. You take the badge with you, get old Bean an' the rangeman an' get down out of here an' stay out,' and walked out the door.

Bean Severn went outside to tell the

rangeman what Twine had said and Bailey, chewing a straw and leaning on a corral stringer nodded without comment until Bean thought they should get the horses, then Jess Bailey nodded again, but still did not move.

Bean was exasperated. As he hiked into the night he said to himself, 'Cowboys! Thick as oak an' twice as lazy.'

Stiles came out, saw his brother at the corral and walked over. 'Will that medicine you give her kill her?'

Twine faced around. 'No; not that I ever heard. Why?'

'Because she's fadin' fast an' I don't think her eyes focus.'

Twine headed for the cabin with long strides. Joe Stiles was correct, the old woman, who had recognized him before, did not see him now. She looked steadily at the rotting old overhead log rafters.

He leaned to feel the side of her neck. There was a pulse, but an erratically weak one. He straightened up when

Cal Lott walked over and looked down. Lott said, 'Before morning, boys,' and walked away. On his stalk past the table he considered the badge, but left it where it was.

A short time later when Stiles went outside, Cal Lott was waiting. 'You stopped that stage?' he asked.

The 'breed shook his head.

'Twine did it?'

'No.'

'Then who?'

'My mother did it.'

Lott snorted derisively. 'You can do better'n that. She couldn't make the trip down there an' back let alone stop the coach.'

Joe Stiles stood a silent moment regarding the larger and heavier man before speaking. 'It don't matter what you believe, mister. She did it. Passed out, fell off her horse an' was lyin' in the mud when Mister Abbot found her — an' the box.'

The rugged storekeeper stood regarding Stiles without a sound before he walked purposefully in the direction of the house.

A man Stiles had never seen before materialized out of the night, spun the 'breed and knocked him senseless with a pistol barrel. He then dragged the 'breed behind the cabin and left him there.

Jess Bailey had leaned on the corral watching without a sound until the stranger appeared from out back, then all he said was, 'The box's in the house,' and the dark shadow retorted, 'Tell me again, you're sure it's three thousand dollars?'

Bailey nodded. 'It warn't no secret in Jefferson.'

They walked together to the house, Bailey entered first. Those inside barely acknowledged his presence until the second rangeman appeared, closed the door and cocked a six-gun; not an especially loud sound, but one once heard never mistaken for anything other than what it was.

Cal Lott stood like a stone statue.

Twine Fourch turned slowly from the bedside.

Cal Lott found his tongue and addressed Jess Bailey, 'What in the hell do you think you're doing?'

Bailey's sidearm was still holstered. He spoke to his companion without looking away from the storekeeper. 'It's yonder by the table.' His voice barely carried. Except that the room was totally silent it wouldn't have.

The rangeman with the cocked Colt sidled past Bailey, kept his gun aimed as he moved towards the table, found the moneybox and hoisted it to the table. He showed a triumphant smile. Jess Bailey was expressionless as finally he drew his six-gun and jerked his head.

His friend got as far as the door with the box under one arm before Bean Severn broke the silence. He knew the stranger. 'Mr Morgan won't like two of his riders turnin' out to be outlaws.'

The man holding the moneybox regarded Bean Severn calmly. 'Tell him we got tired of twelve dollars a month and found.'

After the stranger was gone, Bean addressed Jess Bailey. 'I always wondered about you two.'

If he had intended to elaborate he didn't get the chance. Jess Bailey shot the old scout from a distance of about ten feet. The impact was close enough to the fire for Severn's blood to coagulate almost immediately. It was a good shot; at that distance a blind man could have done as well. Severn's heart was blown to shreds.

Only the old woman neither flinched nor stiffened. She probably didn't hear the shot.

Bailey eyed the men. 'Now you got one less tracker,' he said, and backed into the doorway before speaking again. 'Stay in here for half an hour. Poke your noses out an' I'll shoot them off.'

Twine loosened first, glanced at Bean Severn, went over, dragged the body further from the fire and looked at Cal Lott.

'Did you know them?'

Lott nodded. 'They ride for Will Morgan. They been comin' back each season for several years.' Lott sagged at the table. 'I've visited with Jess Bailey many times when he'd come in with a buckboard for supplies.' Lott glanced where his moneybox had been and softly said, 'I'll be damned.'

It occurred to Twine that his brother had been outside and headed for the door. Two things delayed him, one, the old woman had a coughing fit, the other thing was Cal Lott saying, 'Don't open that door!'

Twine went to the bedside, stroked the woman's throat until the coughing stopped and her eyes focused on him. She smiled, and died.

Cal Lott gingerly opened the door. Nothing happened. He listened. There was no sound. He opened the door wider, fisted his sidearm and looked out and around.

Twine spoke bitterly from beside the cot. 'They're long gone. Find my brother . . . she's dead.'

The storekeeper found Joe Stiles by the noise he was making floundering behind the house, helped him stand and got sticky blood on his hands. When he asked what happened the 'breed did not say a word. He braced against the log wall with one hand and felt his head. The pain was both inside and outside. He started groping his way toward the front wall and the doorway. Cal Lott would have helped but Stiles snarled at him.

Stiles braced against both sides of the doorway. For the second time his shirt front was bloody. This time he looked as unsteady as he had the other time he'd bled.

He got as far as the bench and sat. Cal Lott went after the whiskey. Twine stood like a carving saying nothing until his brother had downed some whiskey and turned to speak. Twine spoke first.

'She's dead.'

Stiles wiped off blood with a bandanna

Cal Lott had handed him. He let the soggy handkerchief fall into his lap, looked first at Twine, then at the old woman, and fell off the bench unconscious.

The storekeeper spoke quietly. 'It'd have been Bailey or the other one,' and seemingly without effort lifted Stiles, placed him atop the table and shook his head without speaking.

Two dead, one knocked out on the floor and one who looked close to dying. He seemed to have forgotten his driving, fierce motivation for being up here.

He sank down on the bench gazing straight ahead with his back to Twine and the cot. He'd lost his moneybox; if there was a possibility of getting it back . . . He twisted on the bench to speak in an awed tone of voice.

'All this for a lousy three thousand dollars?'

Twine didn't speak. He gently pulled a blanket over his mother's face and knelt. He wasn't a praying man; he didn't have to be, he had a soul that did that for him. As he was arising the corralled paint horse nickered. Twine started for the door drawing his six-gun as he went.

Cal Lott started to warn him against opening the door and being back-grounded by candlelight, but Twine got outside before Lott could speak.

He arose and, moving like an old man, went after the whiskey and a dented tin cup. He didn't know what else to do. Pouring whiskey into Joe Stiles or whatever his name was, came close to being an effort in futility. Stiles only swallowed when instinct required it, otherwise some of the whiskey spilled on his sodden shirt. Justin Abbot was moaning and rolling back and forth trying to sit up. Cal helped him to sit up and offered him whiskey also.

Daylight was coming when Twine left the area of the cabin and for the second time lately rode in the wrong direction; he went northward toward the face of Stone Mountain assuming the pair of renegade rangemen had gone in that direction.

They hadn't; they had ridden southward in the direction of the Morgan ranch yard where their possessions were in the bunkhouse.

The first rays of sunlight showed him his error. There were neither tracks nor disturbed earth.

He was close enough to the cliff face to make out a faint, crooked trail. He followed it despite the fact that there were no shod-horse marks, and came into sight of a blackened cave opening.

There was a stone fire ring just beyond the opening. It had ash from a nearby neatly stacked half cord of dry wood.

Horses had been here, their droppings were prominent. There wasn't much graze but there was browse, something horses would eat if there was no graze. There was also a painstakingly built rock corral little more than waist high with its north wall the cliff face.

Somewhere there had to be a spring or a creek. He looked for neither, left his horse tethered and entered the cave. He did not explore to its depths, he didn't have to. Abundant evidence told him two people had lived here. One sleeping place had old tan army blankets, the other sleeping place had cured hides, hairside turned inward.

The imprints of moccasined feet were everywhere. It seemed as though the cave expected its inhabitants to return. Twine took a worn-smooth rosary from its twig, stuck into a crevice, went back outside and stood gazing southward, the only direction with an excellent miles-long view.

He sat on a large flat rock outside the cave, evidently rolled there as a chair. The old rosary had faint inscriptions he couldn't read. They were in French.

There were times in a man's life when, alone and pensive, something vague, almost ethereal came to him. For Twine Fourch this was such a time. It was as though his mother was beside or to one side of him, smiling. He had only seen her smile twice at the cabin. There may have been other times, but he had no such recollection.

A rider was coming. When he appeared, Twine had difficulty accepting his appearance. His face was puffy, his shirt was torn and caked with dried blood. He saw Twine, neither nodded nor spoke until he'd penned the paint horse, then he said, 'I got to lie down,' and halfway to the cave's entrance he collapsed.

Twine found a deer-gut water bag and washed his brother's face. They barely resembled each other. If there had been whiskey — or the little blue bottle — it would have helped.

As it turned out Joe Stiles neither opened his eyes nor moved for more than an hour by which time the sun was overhead.

Twine helped him sit up, propped his back with a bent knee and said, 'No sign of 'em up here.'

Stiles answered huskily, 'They went south,' and looked at his darker brother. 'You couldn't read sign if it was in your face. Twine? She wanted to be buried here, close off the opening with rocks.'

'All right. I'll do it.'

'No you won't. She didn't know you. I'll do it. There's somethin' in there I'll bury with her.'

Twine held up the worn rosary and his brother nodded. 'You found it,' he said, and took the rosary from Twine, held it gently as he also said, 'All this for a moneybox,' and fainted.

Stiles did not regain consciousness until long after he'd been carried inside and placed on the army-blanket bed, and even then his voice wasn't strong.

He said, 'Half-breed Constable. Did you ever try to find us?'

Twine hadn't and did not reply.

'I thought you didn't. She said you would — someday. It turned out she was right.'

Twine remained silent.

'Go on back where you belong. Track down those rangemen. That's your job.'

Twine finally broke his silence. 'In time. I'll get them.'

'If you do, it was that rat-faced one hit me from behind.' Stiles tried to smile. It was a grimace.

'Kill him for me. If you don't I got to find him myself. No whiskey, huh?'

Twine shook his head. 'Where's water?'

'Behind us in a crack in the cliff. The horses need some. Twine, I'll be here when you get back.'

Twine didn't doubt that. His brother was in about as bad a shape as a man could be. He went to find water and care for the horses.

5

A Warm Trail

By the time he got back to the cabin the moon was high and the cabin was vacant except for the old woman, and someone had covered her completely.

He lighted the pair of candles. By their soft brightness he saw something on the table. His badge. Evidently the storekeeper, despite their fight, had relented. Disagreeable old son of a bitch, it was about time he grew up.

Twine didn't pin the badge in place, he put it in his pocket. Because there wasn't a second corpse he assumed they had taken Bean Severn back to Jefferson with them.

From what his brother had said he was sure Stiles would come for their mother when he was able; in a few days probably, and Twine understood

Stiles's quick objection when Twine had offered to help bury the old woman.

He was dog tired. All the whiskey was gone, but the little blue bottle was on the shelf. He neither needed it nor tasted it; he went out where his hobbled horse was eating, bedded down under the stars and neither heard nor saw anything until the following morning when the sun was climbing.

He washed at the creek, decided hunger could wait, rigged up and rode southward.

His appearance in Jefferson was met with neither a welcome nor disapproval over his long absence. At old Severn's burial and for days afterwards Cal Lott told and retold the story. He did this without embellishments; he was not the kind to add colour. His voice only hardened when he came to the end of the tale. How he had lost the moneybox and its contents.

Twine only lingered in the settlement until he felt comfortable about leaving, and this time he told the blacksmith's helper, a large, powerful man named Andy Loftus, to keep order until he returned.

The Morgan ranch was something like eight miles from the settlement and its owner, Wilford — called simply Will — Morgan was a widower with two grown sons. He was likeable and liked. He met Twine Fourch at the tie rack in front of the barn and dispensed with the customary pleasantries to say, 'They got their gatherings some time in the night. We never saw 'em again. Jess Bailey come back every spring for somethin' like six years. He was a good hand. His partner, John Carlile was — different. Never did any more'n he absolutely had to. They partnered up for years. Jess was a good worker. I had trouble believing what Cal Lott told me, not that I figured John was above doin' somethin' like that, but Jess, well, no; that surprised me.'

Morgan made a wry smile. 'I guess it's right a man never really knows folks.'

Twine wasn't interested in abstractions. 'Tell me where they might go.'

Morgan was thoughtfully quiet for a moment before answering. 'I can tell you that Jess came from Pineville, but John was not a man who talked about himself. You know where Pineville is?'

Twine knew, thanked Will Morgan and rode out of his yard. Morgan leaned on the tie rack for some time before shaking his head and crossing the yard to his house. An old shaggy dog too stiff to arise, wagged its tail. He leaned to scratch its back as he told the old dog, who was going deaf, that he wouldn't want that big 'breed on his trail.

Pineville was a two-day ride, something like thirty miles from Jefferson south-westerly. It throve because the railroad had a siding at Pineville and before that, with four intersecting roadways, good dirt for miles and abundant water. Its population, close in and further out, had been steadily increasing for years.

It was located in an incorporated area, the County of Bridger, so it had a sheriff instead of a town marshal or a constable. It even had an apothecary and a dressmaker along with two churches and four saloons.

The liveryman was grizzled, shrewd and had little, piggy, blue eyes. He appraised the big 'breed as Twine turned in to have his animal cared for. The liveryman's name was Archibald Kettle. He was called Arch or just plain Kettle. He had a limp, the result of thinking he could ride a fighting wild stallion. He had stayed aboard two jumps. The third one sent him flying like a bird. He had landed on his right hip; it had required a year to heal and he limped.

The doctor in Pineville diagnosed several bone fractures for which he could do nothing but supply laudanum for pain.

Arch Kettle went through the motions of caring for Twine's big horse and talked at the same time; he knew a stranger — and a 'breed Indian — when he saw one. First off he offered Twine a horse trade. When that was declined he wanted to show Twine a practically new saddle an itinerant rangeman had hocked to him four years back and had never returned to redeem it.

Twine had a saddle, a Powder River rig; it wasn't new but over the years he'd become warped to it. He declined that trade also.

Then he asked Arch Kettle a question. Did he know anyone named Jess Bailey and the lame man stopped what he was doing to answer. 'Jess Bailey? Known him for years. Him an' his ridin' partner John Carlile. You a friend of Jess?'

Twine thumbed back his hat before answering. 'I was in the country, haven't seen him for a spell an' thought I'd look him up.'

The liveryman limped to a bench and sat before speaking again. 'Haven't seen Jess in a 'coon's age. He goes north every spring for work. Him'n John. He might be at the home place, though. It's owned by his daddy, old Wayne Bailey. Jess leaves in the spring, comes back after shippin' season. He's the oldest. His two sisters'n the old man mind things while he's gone.' Kettle paused to vigorously scratch. 'You know the place, do you?'

'Sure don't.'

'Well, it's due east of here maybe ten miles. Got a big old log on the gate with the brand burnt on it. The brand's S Up And Down.' Kettle grinned, 'For old Wayne's three children an' himself.' Arch Kettle was warming to the 'breed. 'You got a name, friend?'

'Clew Whitmun.'

The liveryman considered the dark 'breed without comment. Clew Whitmun sure as hell wasn't no white man. Twine's stance and expression discouraged comment. The liveryman slapped both legs and got to his feet. 'How long you want me to look after your animal, friend?'

Twine had no idea, but handed over several silver coins when he answered. 'Until you see me comin' — friend.'

Pineville had four cafés, two more eateries than houses of worship, but they shared something with the churches, no matter which place a man patronized, the fare was the same.

After eating, he visited the Star Saloon, evidently a popular waterhole because it had about two dozen patrons and one of them was the sheriff, a youngish man of medium height but put together like a Durham bull. His name was Frank Johnson.

Twine introduced himself as Clew Whitmun and stood the sheriff a round. For a fact, Frank Johnson rarely had to pay for drinks.

He asked the same question he'd asked the liveryman and got the impression folks knew Wayne Bailey and his brood.

The sheriff was casual while the conversation had to do with Jess Bailey and his family, but Twine had no difficulty in picking up on the slightly different way the sheriff mentioned John Carlile.

It wasn't anything in particular, it was the nuances that Johnson used; folks west of the Big River were very careful about denigrating men who followed the everyday routine of putting on their britches first, their boots second and their six-gun last.

If Twine had cared to he could have asked questions. There was someone in Pineville who would willingly talk about John Carlile.

His interest was the Bailey place; first thing the following morning he rode for it.

He had the yard in sight when a tall, rawboned girl with pigtails came out of an arroyo to intercept him. He told her his name was Clew Whitmun and that he'd known her brother. The girl's dead level grey eyes made their appraisal before she said, 'I never heard Jess mention that name.'

Twine smiled. 'Ma'am, names are a dime a dozen.'

She didn't return the smile but she said, 'It'll be close to eatin' time an' Pa will want to meet you. My name's Jane Bailey.'

Twine barely nodded in acknowledgement before he said, 'Is Jess around?'

The leggy girl was gazing in the direction of the tree-shaded ranch yard when she replied. 'He was. Him'n John Carlile.' She boosted her horse over into a lope and with Twine behind a few yards, entered the yard with a whoop.

Twine was looping reins when a large, rawboned man with a shock of white hair and a weathered tan face came from the direction of the main house. His long-legged daughter spoke before the older man was more than halfway to the barn.

'This here is Clew Whitmun, a friend of Jess's.'

The older man extended a large,

work-roughened hand but did not smile. 'He ain't here, Mr Whitmun. Him'n John Carlile went south a coupla days ago. Jess said somethin' about a drive of Texas cattle comin' north. Him'n John figured they could hire on because they know the country.' Wayne Bailey gestured for his daughter to take Twine's horse and care for it as he said, 'Supper time, almost, Mister Whitmun. We got time for a jolt or two.'

Twine watched the girl leading his horse down the barn runway, decided since it was getting late he'd have supper then head in the direction of the Texas cattle drive.

He never made it.

Jane Bailey's sister was dark, almost Mexican looking and quiet. She acknowledged the introduction then went to work in the kitchen. She was still putting a meal together out there while Twine and the older man had a drink of whiskey in the clean but genteelly ragged parlour.

Jane came in, looked at her father,

ignored Twine, went through to the kitchen and helped her sister. Neither of them said a word.

Wayne Bailey was an expansive, friendly individual and talked of the way his son worked out and brought back money. S Up And Down no longer ran very many cattle. The older man said he wasn't able to do much and working cattle wasn't woman's work so he had sold down. He didn't mention his wife for an excellent reason, she had run off with one of those travelling men who used a fringe-top buggy, wore a curly-brim derby hat and a huge diamond stickpin. That had been shortly after the last child had been born. No one had heard of her since.

Jane came to the doorway to announce that supper was ready. Twine followed the older man, stood behind his chair and froze. His lawman's badge was on the dinner plate and Jane was looking unwaveringly at him.

Bailey saw the badge as he was

pulling back the chair to sit down. The dark girl, like her sister, was motionless in place regarding Twine.

Wayne Bailey halted in the act of sitting, slowly looked up and said, 'That thing belong to you, Mister Whitmun?'

Jane replied before Twine could. 'It was in his saddle-bag, Pa.'

Twine made no move to sit. He looked steadily at the leggy girl as he said, 'Is that a habit of yours, goin' through folks's saddle-bags?'

She ignored the question. 'Pa, Jess's in trouble.'

The older man accepted that without change. 'Mr Whitmun, are you a lawman?'

'Yes sir. Up north a few days' ride.'

'An' you want my boy?'

'I want to talk to him.'

'What did he do?'

'Stole a moneybox for openers. Three thousand dollars in it.'

Jane interrupted. 'I had a feelin', Pa, when I met him out yonder.'

The older man ignored that, made a gesture and said, 'Set, Mister whatever-your-name-is.'

Twine sat. Where the tabletop hid movement he gently tugged loose the tie-down over his holstered Colt.

The dark girl saw his shoulder dip and rise, stepped to a rear doorway, picked up a single-barrelled shotgun and aimed it as she said, 'Put the pistol on the table.'

Twine did. The dark girl's father looked at her in mild reproach. 'Folks don't point guns at guests, SaraLee.'

Twine considered the steak and potatoes and the cupful of black java. He was hungry, hadn't eaten since the night before. He picked up his eating implements and went to work on the steak. Both girls were like mute statues, but their father also attacked his meal.

Halfway through he asked Twine a question. 'Anyone get hurt?'

Twine washed down a mouthful before replying. 'An old buffler hunter named Severn. He got killed.'

'He was old?'

'Yes.'

'So'm I, Sheriff. It's not as big a crime when an old man gets killed as when a young one does.'

Twine didn't answer. A person could find a whole army of folks who'd disagree with that.

'How much money did they get?'

'Three thousand dollars.'

The dark girl made an almost silent sigh. Her sister showed no reaction.

Wayne Bailey chewed, swallowed, drank coffee and spoke again as he was putting the cup down. 'Is there a reward, Sheriff?'

'No. Not yet anyway. The money belonged to a storekeeper up in Jefferson.'

'Pretty upset, was he?'

Twine looked at the old man. He didn't make $3,000 a year and from the looks of the Bailey place neither did its owner.

Jane abruptly addressed her father. 'No!'

The dark girl quietly said, 'There's not that many cattle left, Pa.'

Wayne Bailey continued to eat. Near the end of the meal he used a large slice of coarse, homemade bread to sop up the gravy.

Twine's discomfort was abating. Jane had shocked the hell out of him, but that had been a half-hour back. Jess's father held up a cup for a refill, accepted it, cupped it with both hands and spoke without looking at Twine.

'If she knew it'd break his mother's heart. She loved the girls, Sheriff, but Jess was the apple of her eye.' He finally looked up. 'I can find the three thousand dollars for the storeman. About the shot one . . . '

The dark girl went briskly to work clearing the table. Her long-legged sister went to a parlour sideboard and returned with a whiskey bottle and two little jolt glasses.

Neither man touched the bottle. Wayne Bailey quietly said, 'Gawd almighty damn.' SaraLee reproved him.

94

He smiled tiredly at her. 'I know. Well, Sheriff, what I told you was the truth, Jess an' John went south to hire on as guides for a cattle drive.' The older man arose with an effort and left the room. Jane Bailey lit into Twine. He endured the tongue-lashing looking straight at the long-legged girl, arose and went after his hat on the parlour floor. He was heading for the door when the reticent dark girl addressed him from the kitchen doorway.

'If there's no bounty, Sheriff . . . '

'It's my job. Right now I don't feel real good about it but I got to do it.'

'Jess'll fight.'

'Yes, ma'am, sometimes they do.'

'Are you a married man, Sheriff?'

'No, ma'am, an' if you got in mind what I figure you might have, no, thank you.'

His hand was on the latch string when Jane spoke. Her approach was neither quiet nor gentle. She said, 'Jess'n John are both dead shots an' fast.'

Twine nodded gravely about that. 'Like I said before, sometimes they are.'

He passed out on to the porch with its warped overhang. Dusk had settled. Among a scattering of old chairs Wayne Bailey was gently rocking. He spoke without looking around. 'You have children, Sheriff?'

'No, an' I'm not a sheriff, I'm a town constable.'

'I'd guess that, you bein' a 'breed. Sit down for a spell.'

Twine sat.

'You a smokin' man, Constable?'

Twine interpreted that correctly, dug out a not-much-used sack of Durham and handed it over. For as long as was required for the older man to build and light a smoke both men were silent. After the first deep inhalation and exhalation, Wayne Bailey said, 'I give it up thirty years ago; my woman couldn't stand the smell . . . Constable, the boy come to manhood different from either side of the family.'

Twine took a chance. 'There's been other times?'

The reply came slowly. 'I sold down to square things, but there was never before a killing . . . You're goin' to keep goin' until you find him?'

'Yes.'

'Constable, if it comes to guns bury him wherever he dies. Don't bring him home.'

Twine built a quirly and had a coughing fit when he first inhaled. The older man looked around at him. 'That's what happened to me fifty years ago, but I wasn't no quitter. I kept at it until I didn't cough.'

The old man smiled in the quickening darkness. Twine thanked him for his hospitality and went down to the barn for his horse.

6

A New Day

It was a big country. Its inhabitants thought in big terms. A cattle drive up out of Texas made sign anyone could read from high places.

For Twine Fourch the problem was how long had the drovers been on the trail? He had to guess that if Bailey and Carlile knew of such a drive, given the slowness of moccasin telegraph, the drive should be well out of Texas, New Mexico and northward. Those first two places with vast expanses of flat country made cow drives able to make good time. Northerly, they'd encounter mountains and mountain passes which were rarely where they should be so drives were slowed.

His second day out he saw the dust, rising great clouds were visible for fifty miles. It did not have to be the drive he was seeking, but he gambled on that by stopping overnight in a village where the population was at least half Mexican, made certain his horse would be properly cared for, hunted up an eatery and had supper.

Texans, Mexicans and some tribesmen specialized in meals sufficiently garnished with peppers to induce several varieties of internal difficulties after a meal.

Twine was accustomed to meat, potatoes and coffee and baked bread with churned chunks of butter. The eatery in the village where he stopped over had a fat, good-natured Mexican proprietor who, while he was not particularly averse to strangers, nevertheless derived sly pleasure from overloading his *entamotados* with *jalapeños*, not the green ones, the red ones. Twine took two mouthfuls. There were three other diners. He put down his eating utensils, drew his handgun, cocked it and addressed the fat man behind the counter. 'You can do better, friend, or I'll kill you.'

For a long moment the drop of a pin would have sounded like a cannon. The other diners froze, the proprietor did too but very briefly. He swept up the platter, disappeared into his kitchen and returned with a fresh meal on a clean platter. And he smiled ingratiatingly.

'The other is better for you,' he said, and shrugged fleshy shoulders. 'I thought you were like me.'

Twine leathered the sidearm, considered the new meal and said, 'I'm not Messican, friend.'

'Ah; *Indio*.'

After eating, Twine hunted up the man who cared for his horse and offered two bits for the privilege of sleeping in his hay mow.

The proprietor took the coin. 'Mostly,' he told Twine, 'they don't pay, they sneak up there'n I flush 'em out when I go up to pitch feed down. Help yourself.'

He was unable to go directly toward the drive because for two days he saw no dust and despite sashaying east and west neither made a sighting nor heard bawling.

On the fifth day he rode a ridge top from east to west and, where the rocky spine trickled off, he saw dust. Satisfied, he took his time. Drovers bedded their cattle and got settled for a feeding and bedrolls after dark.

He had no plan beyond locating the drive. It was a tad late in the year for large drives to be heading north but it was not unheard of.

The night was glass clear with unnumbered stars. He only stopped when the scent told him he was close, the scent and the bawling of cattle who hadn't been able to eat while being driven and now complained that the men riding nighthawk wouldn't let them spread as much as they wanted to.

He dismounted in darkness, stood at his horse's head and pondered. If this was the wrong drive he had spent nearly a week while the right drive went past, but he was reasonably confident; there were precious few drives north this time of year.

The customary thing would be to ride in, accept the invitation to eat and look for his men. They would, of course, recognize him and if the other drivers liked them . . .

He wandered until he found a stunted tree, looped the reins and left the horse. He could find it in a hurry if he had to, darkness or not. To reach the mealy tree he had crossed a stone field and several ancient deadfalls which had become petrified.

Someone up ahead was playing a harmonica with accompaniment from a Jew's harp. The song was an old one much favoured by Southerners, even second and third generations of them.

'Lorena, the snow is on the ground again.

The days are long my heart is
    sore . . . '

Twine had heard the song before
without any idea that it was an old
Confederate soldier's song.

The musician playing the Jew's harp
stopped, raised his head and held Twine
motionless as he sang.

'*Jos wo na — atz, tow — i . . .* '

He got no further. Twine hadn't
understood, but among the other
riders at the wagon someone called
out, 'Gawddamn bronco, sing it in
Texican.'

A less annoyed man spoke quietly.
'Leave him be. It's a Kiowa song,
means come eat good an' be happy.'

The harmonica player put up his
instrument. There was mumbled talk,
someone pitched wood into the fire and
Twine walked closer looking for faces
he would recognize.

He didn't find them, but they found
him.

A gravelly voice spoke behind him in

the night. 'Mister, you could get hurt sneakin' up on folks.'

Twine turned slowly. The man with the fisted Colt had a thick beard. It was difficult to make out much more in poor light. He addressed Twine again, 'What you doin' skulkin' up on us in the dark? What's your name?'

This time Twine answered truthfully. 'Twine Fourch. I'm lookin' for two men name Bailey and Carlile.'

The bearded man said, 'Are you now? Face forward an' walk. I'll tell you when to stop.'

The fire was dying, two drovers were unrolling their soogans. Altogether there were five of them, counting the whiskered individual with the fisted pistol.

He called ahead, 'Look what I found out yonder skulkin' around. A danged In'ian. Most likely out to steal horses.'

The drovers stood like statues with weak firelight limning them. A rider with a high nasal voice and a Texan voice said, 'Why'n't you disarm the son of a bitch, Rory?'

Whiskers answered curtly. 'You do it.'

The man who removed Twine's gun grinned as he stepped back holding the weapon. 'You ain't all tomahawk, are you?'

'Half,' Twine said, studying the man with his gun. 'I wasn't skulkin', I was lookin' for those two gents across the fire.'

The Texan turned. 'Them two?' he said, and faced forward. 'Are you the law, mister?'

Carlile spoke quickly. 'He's constable to a little place up north. He ain't a real lawman, are you, Mr Fourch?'

Twine didn't answer, he looked steadily across hot coals at the two men he'd been seeking. The whiskered drover named Rory sarcastically said, 'Mr In'ian, you look like a reasonable 'breed. We need them two boys. We don't know the country an' they do. Suppose I was to hand you twenty dollars an' you just up and rode off an' never come back.'

Twine remained silent, his unblinking gaze fixed on Bailey and Carlile. Eventually he addressed Bailey. 'This time your pa don't want you back.'

The drovers considered Twine. Their business was driving cattle, at the end of each day they relaxed around a supper fire. What had abruptly shattered their moment of ease was not a welcome respite after twelve hours in the saddle.

A slim, youthful Texan broke the silence with a question directed at Twine. 'Why do you want 'em, mister?'

'For robbery an' murder.'

The bearded individual came from behind Twine still holding his six-gun in his right fist. He asked who Bailey and Carlile had killed.

Twine's answer was curt. 'An old buffler hunter named Severn.'

'Both of 'em killed him?'

'No. That one, Jess Bailey.'

'An' how much did they rob?'

'Three thousand dollars.'

The bearded man's cheeks puffed out as he exhaled slowly. As the trail boss, Bailey and Carlile were valuable to him. He'd been a drover many years. In strange country his successful deliveries had depended upon competent guides. He had hired Bailey and Carlile on sight when they rode into his camp and convinced him they knew the country all the way to Montana.

He holstered the handgun, perched on the downed tongue of the wagon eyeing Twine as he spoke. 'Mister, we got a long drive ahead an' this late in the season we can't put up with no delays. You understand?'

Twine nodded.

'Well, Sheriff, we can't let you just ride in here an' take our point men away.' The bearded man paused, spat and continued speaking. 'Suppose you ride along with us, an' when we find a place where I can hire another pair of guides, you can have 'em?'

Before Twine could respond, John Carlile said, 'Rory, he's a town constable.

Not even a county sheriff. He's got no authority here.'

An older rider nodded his head while regarding Twine but he said nothing.

Jess Bailey spoke next. 'We didn't kill nobody an' we never stole no money.'

The trail boss considered Carlile and Bailey, spat again and eased up off the wagon tongue facing Twine. 'You heard the man, Constable. You can trail with us until we can find another point man then you'n them can settle your difference.'

As though to emphasize that this ended the discussion, the bearded man expectorated again before finally saying, 'If you're hungry, help yourself.'

A voice Twine recognized immediately spoke from the darkness. 'Empty their holsters, Mr Whitmun.' This statement was accompanied by the sound of someone levering a cartridge into a Winchester barrel.

No one moved. No one was more surprised than Twine Fourch. The youthful cowboy looked in the direction of the trail boss when he said, 'It's a danged woman, Rory.'

The gunshot explosion not only prevented an answer, it kicked coals from the fire in the direction of the youthful drover's feet and legs. He jumped.

The body-less voice in the darkness spoke again. 'Next one's through your gizzard. *Shuck them pistols!*'

The bearded trail boss was the first to obey. He was not a coward, but neither was he a fool.

As the guns fell, Twine twisted slightly to look behind, but darkness and flourishing chaparral prevented him from seeing her. He straightened back around.

The trail boss spoke sourly. 'That your wife, Constable?'

Twine said, 'No.'

'Well, mister, you sure's hell got a guardian angel.'

Twine looked across the dying fire at Jess Bailey who had probably also recognized his sister's voice. Neither

Bailey nor John Carlile showed any expression until the invisible girl said, 'Jess, you'n John get on your horses an' *git*!'

Twine loosened, watched Bailey and Carlile turn their back on him and stride in the direction of the remuda's rope corral. Without looking back he said, 'Ma'am, you're puttin' yourself in a right bad position. Aidin' an' abettin' fugitives to escape makes you just as guilty as they are.'

She did not respond until they could all clearly hear running horses. She waited until the sound was no longer audible then addressed Twine.

'You know why I did this. Get on your horse and don't look back.'

He started to speak and was interrupted by the bearded trail boss. 'That's good advice she give you. Right now I'm in the mood to hang you. Get the hell away from here. If I ever see you again . . . '

For Twine, hours of saddle-backing, missing meals and sleep to achieve success, was ruined on a dark night among drovers who were looking at him as though he was a sidewinder.

He went directly to his horse, got astride and turned back the way he had come. If Jane Bailey was trailing him he neither knew nor cared, but he doubted it. The further he rode the more he wondered at her ability to dog him without him being aware she was doing it.

He found no excuse for what she had done, brother or not. He and book law had not always agreed, but the oath he had taken to uphold it mattered. Among most people on both sides of his heritage integrity mattered, even if he had not to his knowledge ever heard the word.

He bedded down in the chilly pre-dawn. His horse browsed in hobbles although restraints weren't necessary. Twine Fourch and his horse were old friends; he took the best care of it he could, in return it gave him loyalty.

The first settlement he encountered

was a clutch of mud buildings in the middle of a sea of dead grass, huge rocks and an occasional tree. It was called Beaufort. It had a combination eatery, pool hall and saloon. There was a cramped adobe which housed a general store. There were three public corrals in the middle of the place and among them was an adobe and rock building no larger than an ordinary kitchen which was presided over by a dark fat man of Mexican descent named Antonio Morro. Morro did not use the customary Mexican custom of a letter 'y' meaning 'and' followed by his mother's name. The reason was simple: his mother had been Mojave full blood.

His brother, Roberto Morro, owned and operated the trading and livery business with its office in another half-adobe, half-rock building.

When Twine Fourch dismounted out front, Roberto, who was also overweight and who sweated copiously even during winter, appeared smiling broadly. There

112

was an unmentioned affinity among 'breeds, most of them anyway.

Twine followed him to a high-walled adobe corral, saw his horse turned in and said he wanted it both hayed and grained, to which the heavier and shorter man agreed. He watched Twine head for the eatery, waited a few minutes, then hiked up to the *clabozo* to tell his brother a stranger had ridden in and in Roberto's opinion he was either an outlaw of some kind or a lawman.

The Beaufort saloon, pool hall, café was large, gloomy and unkempt. Its proprietor was a skinny, hawk-faced man named Buster Munzer, assumed by the locals to be 1) an army deserter, 2) a person who had abandoned a family somewhere or 3) a fugitive. He had been in Beaufort eleven years. He spoke Spanish not out of choice, but because those who didn't neither understood or were understood. He made a not uncommon error, he mistook Twine Fourch to be half Mex.

113

The eatery section of the big old former Mexican barracks had been a mess hall and hundreds of years of the same odours had soaked in and saturated the adobe walls.

Two older women appeared to take his order. The moment he spoke English one of the women left the room.

What he wanted as much as food was information about Jane Bailey. She had to have stopped somewhere on her way home, or wherever she went.

He thought she might have known where her brother and Carlile would head for. He would track her starting the following morning.

It didn't happen. He didn't do it.

He was sleeping like a dead man in his soogan with the moon well down, when someone struck him a sweeping blow. Even as a child Twine Fourch had been a light sleeper. He moved to sit up and reach for the coiled shellbelt at the same moment she said, 'It was a scorpion. A big one with its tail poised.'

He pulled back his right arm, got straighter, looked stonily at her and shook his head. Along with being an accessory she was some kind of witch or ghost.

He scratched his head. 'What in hell? You did your work.'

She was hunkering, the saw handle of her holstered Colt outlined in poor light. 'It's a big country down here. I was lonesome.'

It was such a patent prevarication he smiled. 'All right, now you go home.'

'I can't do that until you pass me your word you won't stay after my brother.'

'Ma'am, your brother shot an' killed a man in cold blood.'

'Back at that cow camp they said you didn't have no lawman authority down here.'

Twine watched the irate large scorpion heading for his feet, leaned, scuffed dirt in its face and it went blindly off in a different direction.

She said, 'You're after the bounty.'

He looked steadily at her. 'I'm after no such thing an' it don't matter where it happened, it's murder.'

She changed position, crossed long legs and sat like an Indian regarding him. In a sarcastic tone she said, 'Clew Whitmun.'

He replied dryly, 'I knew a feller years back named that. They hung him for shootin' a man an' his wife.'

'What's your real name?'

'Twine Fourch.'

'That's ugly,' she stated, glanced at the position of the sinking moon and said, 'Are you going to stay in Beaufort?'

'You know I'm not. Ma'am, you'll lie but I got to ask you: where did they go?'

'Mr Fourch, I don't lie. Not to anyone. I don't know where they went, but I'd guess it'll be so far from down here you'll never find them.'

A horse nickered and was answered

by another horse. She arose, dusted off her britches and said, 'I'll ride with you for a spell.'

He slept fully clothed but without his hat, boots and shellbelt. She handed him the hat and boots and waited.

He swore to himself, rolled out, dumped the hat on and stamped into his boots. When they were facing each other he said, 'You don't ride with me.'

She put her head slightly to one side as she replied, 'As far as the turnoff to home. I'll bring the horses in.' As she was movin' away she also said, 'My name's Jane, not ma'am, and you know it.'

7

On the Trail

There were problems when people of the opposite sex spent hours in the saddle together. Jane Bailey shocked Twine Fourch when the sun was high by saying, 'I'll step into them big rocks for a spell. All you got to do is stand on the far side of your horse.'

That is exactly what he did by keeping his back to the rocks. When they were ready to resume riding he said, 'You're different for a female woman.'

'Different from other women you've known?'

'I expect so, only I haven't known many.'

'How about your mother?'

He turned slowly to regard her. 'You ask an awful lot of questions for someone who should know better.' For a while they rode in silence looking at distant heat-hazed mountains. He eventually said, 'She's dead,' and changed the subject. 'What did your pa say when you told him you figured to follow me?'

'I left about one in the morning without even telling my sister an' we never had secrets from each other. Do you have sisters, or maybe brothers?'

'I have a brother. I had a sister. She died when she was little.' He turned on her irritably. 'Don't ask personal questions. Was you raised in a barn?'

She didn't take umbrage; she changed the subject. 'Where are you going?'

He was still irritable when he replied, 'Wherever the damned trail takes me. With you, as far as the turnoff to your home.'

He hadn't hastened going south nor did he hasten on the return trip. Jane Bailey passed the time talking about herself and her family since her curiosity about him had been cut off.

She told him of her sister and brother, how her father had sold cattle to get Jess out of scrapes, something Twine had deduced on the porch that evening with Wayne.

She also told about growing up, about a neighbour boy inviting her to go riding with him and how he had acted until she abruptly turned and loped back home.

Her life had been interesting to her. It interested Twine only because he had to listen. His thoughts were about her brother and his rat-faced riding partner.

By the time they had bypassed Jefferson village some miles to the west he was looking forward to parting company with her.

When they intersected the wagon ruts leading in the right direction and he drew rein, she said, 'You won't find them as easy as you did before. They know more rat-hole hideouts than you can guess.'

He sat his saddle regarding her when

he said, 'No thanks, if you're hintin' I can't find 'em on my own, and you got chores at home. What'll your pa think, you being gone so long?' Something he hadn't noticed before: she had a faint sprinkling of freckles.

She leaned on the saddlehorn looking at him. 'Mr Fourch, the man you're after is my brother.'

No retort was required so he nodded at her.

'Well, us Baileys is close and we don't take kindly to some bounty hunter after one of us.'

Twine was tiring of this, he wanted to be on his way. 'I'm not a bounty hunter. I'm a lawman after a pair of . . . '

'My brother is not an outlaw!'

He studied her expression briefly, lifted his rein hand and snugged his mount with his knees. It began walking.

The following day he ran across that county sheriff named Frank Johnson riding alone some distance from Pineville. Where they met was near a bosque of shade trees of which they took advantage. The sheriff asked if Twine had found what he'd been looking for and because Twine didn't want to waste time explaining what he had been through, he simply said, 'I saw 'em, they run for it an' now I got to start all over.'

Sheriff Johnson, leaning on his saddlehorn, looked hard over Twine's right shoulder and said, 'I could be wrong but I think there's someone followin' you.'

Twine twisted to look back. He saw trees, brush, miles of graze and browse with no movement in any of it.

As he straightened forward he sighed. 'A ghost,' he said, brushed the brim of his hat and rode on.

He was tempted to look back but restrained himself.

He sashayed eastward seeking shod-horse sign and found a lot more than he needed until he was a considerable distance into the cattle country. He paused at a stone trough to tank up his horse and saw reasonably fresh imprints in the moist mud where two riders had done as he was doing, had watered their horses.

Because these were the only sign of shod horses he'd seen away from settlements and they headed north after the drinking had been 'tended to, he tracked, not convinced he was on the right trail, but on a north-south line it was the best he had.

Eventually he was in country he was familiar with. The tracks veered westerly to the road and here tracking was more difficult, most riders rode shod horses and a travelled trace inevitably had plenty of sign. Most of it pointed southward. More than one set of sign also showed riders going down country in the direction of Jefferson, which should have been discouraging but wasn't for a simple reason: among tracks heading northward there was only one double set of two riders travelling together.

If Twine hadn't been hoping very

hard he was following the right sign, it might have occurred to him that many men, neighbours or friends, rode together.

It might also have crossed his mind that with unpleasant recollections of the territory north of Jefferson, the men he sought might have ridden in any one of three other directions, or had ridden miles east of the Stone Mountain country. The place would be as haunted to them as it was to Twine.

On a trail Twine Fourch tracked, he rarely deflected, and since the trail he had found now fitted his requirements for Bailey and Carlile he would stay on it.

He had been overly zealous other times. There was a fifty-fifty chance he was doing the same thing this time.

He bedded down before dusk with a clear view of Stone Mountain ahead and to his left. He thought of the old woman and his brother. They were as different from him as night was from day, but the old woman had been mother to them both and bloodties were important.

When dusk settled he had been following an angling trail. It made no sense for him to think he knew where Bailey and Carlile were heading. That old log house up yonder with its tumbledown rock corral would be the last place he'd figure they'd head for. In their boots he wouldn't have gone up there. On the other hand, with a lawman hunting them, the Stone Mountain country would be an excellent place to hide in. There were hundreds of miles of darkly haunted canyons, excellent high places to watch a back trail.

When he hobbled the horse in a tall stand of wild oats and unrolled his soogan near a second growth fir tree, he bedded down unable to think of a single reason why his prey would return to an area where they could have only bad recollections.

This night there was a nearly full

moon highlighting an eerie primitive landscape to which he paid little attention.

He was hungry again, which was no novelty, and he was weary, otherwise he might have heeded his horse's rigidly attentive stance with wild oat stalks protruding from both sides of its mouth.

Sleep arrived almost before he had shed his boots, hat and gun-belt. He had no idea how long he had been asleep when his horse nickered, a noise which sound sleepers rarely heard, but Twine heard it, leaned to fist the holstered Colt and waited. The horse did not nicker a second time, but that did not have to be significant. Horses trumpeted with reason, they softly nickered only when they had a friendly scent.

Twine was perfectly still lying on his back with the gun-hand across his stomach. It was too long a wait, he fell asleep again.

The next time he awakened there

was a sickly colour to the sky except in the east where several layers of diluted red presaged the arrival of dawn's first light.

It was cool without being chilly and somewhere not too distant a bird made garrulous sounds and got no answer. Twine was in no hurry to roll out. His horse came close and solemnly eyed the bedroll briefly then hobble-hopped where there was feed.

He was rested but not entirely bright-eyed and bushy-tailed. He stamped into his boots, dropped his hat on and was leaning for the gun-belt when his horse nickered again and this time Twine straightened up, belt in hand, to follow out the direction in which his horse was looking.

There was no movement, just some trees, night shadows and thick stands of thornpin brush. He gazed in the direction of the mountain where daylight was beginning to splash across the higher elevations.

A saddleless, bridleless horse, grey

and flat-chinned came out of a stand of brush, eyed Twine briefly before walking without haste in the direction of Twine's animal. The old horse was long past the neck-bowing, pawing and snorting age and Twine's animal had never been on the prod. They smelled noses then went to browsing as though they were old friends.

Twine recognized the horse. How it happened to be up where its owner had been killed, bareback and unbridled, was a minor mystery.

Bean Severn had a log corral behind his house down in Jefferson. Evidently whoever had inherited Bean's old horse didn't have a good corral or had forgotten to close a gate.

Twine rolled his blankets, lashed them behind the cantle, went out to remove hobbles and bring his horse close to be rigged out. Bean Severn's old animal watched all this but made no move to get closer.

Twine was ready to strike camp when the old horse looked over its shoulder and whinnied. Twine, on the left side ready to mount, leaned on the saddle seat scanning. For a while there was nothing to see or hear, but, as he was putting a foot into the stirrup, one hand on the horn, the left hand with reins in it holding mane hair, a rider came around a big, high sticker-bush and smiled.

'Good morning, Mr Manhunter.'

He stood like a stork with one foot in the bucket and neither spoke nor shifted his gaze. Jane Bailey rode closer, swung to the ground and, trailing her reins, said, 'Do you know that old horse? He was coming up this way from Jefferson. When it got too dark I followed him. Was he raised up here or something? He never changed course, led me to this spot like he knew what he was doing.'

Twine put both feet on the ground as he leaned across leather to say, 'I told you go home.'

'I went home, cleaned up, took a fresh horse and tracked you. Mr

Fourch, I know what you're doing. I saw two sets of tracks, too.'

'Ma'am, do everyone a favour an' go home.'

'Mr Fourch, I told you, it's Jane, not ma'am. Pineville's a long way from here and I already told you I'm not going to leave off so you can kill my brother.'

'I figure to arrest him, not kill him.'

She did what she often did, she changed the subject. While she was looking northward she said, 'What's up there besides that bird-face mountain, my brother?'

The sun was well up. As far as Twine knew there was no need for haste, but he had no intention of standing there talking to Jane Bailey so he answered her question curtly as he moved to mount up.

'It's a long story; you likely wouldn't be interested an' I got things to do. Jane, go home.'

She waited until he was astraddle, evening up his reins before speaking again. 'That's where the buffalo hunter was killed?'

'Yes . . . Jane, don't trail me.'

He left her standing there, convinced his last admonition had been a pure waste of breath. For a fact she was good at reading sign and stealth. He'd had no idea she stayed home when she went there, if she did. She had; where else would she get clean clothes?

He was picking his way through forest giants when he reached a pint-sized clearing and looked back. There was no sign of her.

He shook his head and continued on his way, found the old trail and stayed on it following the same two sets of shod-horse marks he'd been following, more convinced than ever that, for whatever reason he had no idea, Bailey and Carlile were up ahead, maybe at the old log house or possibly further up, near the cliff or possibly in some hideout they knew of elsewhere. The Stone Mountain country had dozens of areas where two men and their animals could stay lost for years.

He had the old cabin in sight when he thought of his brother. Joe would be no match for Bailey and Carlile even if he knew they were coming. But Joe would know every hideout place.

The old house looked the same from the outside. It now had a brooding appearance which could have been Twine's imagination. Two people had died there, one violently, the other for no reason except being worn out.

He left the ruts and worked his way around among the trees. The tracks didn't go to the cabin. Possibly Bailey and Carlile felt no more urgency than Twine felt to go over there.

The tracks made a big sashay from east to north and around westerly. They led down behind the old corral where stalks of cured hay indicated that two horses had been fed here, then they continued completing their three-quarter course around the house.

Twine was satisfied. With no inkling why the outlaws had returned to this place he was satisfied they had and that they were somewhere not too distant. He had one of two choices: tie his horse and go manhunting on foot, or go north to the cliff face and see if his brother was alone up there.

He chose the latter course, veered away from the tracks and rode due northerly. He was more than halfway when the scent of wood smoke satisfied his anxiety of Joe not being up there.

Before entering the browsed-off place he saw the cave. It had been masterfully concealed by rock work which sealed off every inch of the opening. Within a few years the closure would look like the rest of the cliff.

He dismounted, stood beside his horse and made a night-bird whistle. He had to repeat it three times before there was movement south-westerly where sunlight didn't reach and his brother moved into sight between two large fir trees. Joe had a Winchester held loosely as though he had been hunting, which he had. Anyone living as Joe Stiles lived supported himself off the land, not just for meat although that would be a mainstay but also for wild onions, wild apples and edible small plants.

Joe neither waved nor spoke. He stood considering Twine for a long moment before walking out of the gloom toward him.

He made a careless hand sign, looked steadily at Twine and said, 'Why'd you come back?' and gestured in the direction of the rocked-up cave front. 'She'll lie in there until she turns to dust. Did you come back to help me with her?'

Twine didn't answer the question, he said, 'You remember those two renegade rangemen, Bailey and Carlile?'

Joe nodded. 'That's who it is. I didn't get close enough to see 'em good. Why'd they come back?'

'Damned if I know, Joe. Do you know where they are?'

'I know where they were. That was yestiddy about this time. Twine, who's the other one, the one ridin' a big puddin'-footed sorrel horse?'

Twine audibly sighed. 'Jane Bailey, sister to Jess Bailey. She's been followin' me because she thinks I want to kill her brother. Where did you see her?'

'Comin' up the old ruts from a distance. I didn't know it was a woman.' Joe leaned on his Winchester considering his brother. 'Why would Bailey an' Carlile come back up here?'

Twine had no idea but he had a suggestion. 'I found 'em in a drovers' camp down south. Their sister dogged me from behind an' let them escape. I read their sign and the girl read my sign.'

Joe calmly said, 'We can ambush her at the cabin. She may be a good tracker but the way she was ridin', out in plain sight, I'd guess she's not very *coyote* about skulkin'. You want to catch her?'

At the present time the last thing Twine wanted was another meeting with Jane Bailey. He dryly said, 'She'll talk your arm off.'

Joe, who seemed not to know how to smile, grinned at Twine. 'Let's go.'

'Joe, first off I'd like to know Bailey and Carlile aren't goin' to bushwhack us. We can leave her wanderin' around. Far as I know she's harmless, but her brother an' his partner sure aren't.'

Joe Stiles was agreeable. He turned without another word and walked back the way he had come, into the eternal gloom of a primeval forest.

It was difficult to estimate the time of day in an area where fir tips seemed almost intertwined, but it was mid-afternoon and the wild inhabitants of the timber uplands noisily scattered in all directions at the scent and sighting of a pair of two-legged things, one carrying a killing stick.

Joe's footgear left no tracks and barely made imprints where generations of fir needles made the ground spongy to walk over. But Twine's boots scuffed enough places to make him easy to track.

Joe didn't halt until they came to a small lightning-cleared grassy place which was empty but which had cropped-off seed heads where large meat animals had grazed.

Joe changed course. Twine guessed they were going south-east. It was a good guess considering Twine, like most people, lost a sense of direction in an area of close-spaced big trees. Joe intended to bring them up behind the cabin, but from a discreet forest-gloom distance.

He told Twine that this area was where he had last seen Bailey and Carlile.

8

Getting Crowded

What caught Twine's attention was a swift, swishing movement. He brushed Joe's arm and jutted his jaw.

Joe led off, more carefully from here on until they saw two dozing horses tethered to low tree limbs. Both saddles had empty saddle boots. Whoever owned those horses had taken Winchesters with them.

Joe made a protracted study before leaning to softly ask Twine if Bailey and Carlile could know he was tracking them.

Twine's answer was cryptic. 'Most likely. They know by now I don't give up.'

The answer satisfied Joe who said, 'Where are they?'

The answer to that required cruising,

looking for boot tracks which should be clear. What Joe eventually found was a pair of tracks skirting southward away from the old house. His brother swore under his breath. 'Sure as hell they've seen her.'

Joe didn't argue. 'A blind man could have seen her ridin' up the ruts.'

They resumed reading sign until the men who had left it sashayed closer to the final tree fringe where ancient rotting stumps told their own story. This was where the cabin's builder had cut down his logs.

Joe Stiles was puzzled. From their latest position they could see the old ruts very clearly and there was no sign of the girl. Joe made a guess. 'If she's as good a tracker as you said, she's more'n likely picked up your tracks.'

Twine had some brief uncharitable thoughts before he nudged his brother. 'Keep goin'. Like I said she's not important, her brother is.'

Joe quartered to pick up the sign. It led him back toward the south side of the log house. Where it ended was over at the house. Joe had to guess about that because he had no intention of exposing them both by crossing the cleared area.

He told Twine he didn't believe the outlaws would still be at the house. He based this on how old the sign was that he and Twine had been following.

He was mistaken, which was excusable since they could only see the back of the house and a silver of the southerly wall.

A man cursing with feeling settled the matter of Bailey and Carlile not being at the cabin. Not just cursing but speaking angrily at the top of his voice.

'What in the hell do you think you're doin'? How come you to be up here? Jane, being snoopy'll get you killed someday. Get off that horse an' come inside.'

Joe faced his brother. 'Like I said, a good tracker but not real *coyote*.'

Twine wasn't interested. Finally, on

his second manhunt, he knew where his fugitives were.

He mumbled aloud. 'Forted up in there.'

Joe was less troubled. 'There's nothin' left. I took the food, the old table, the bench and the old woman's bed. Twine, you don't expect there's somethin' hid in there, do you? What about the moneybox?'

'They left the moneybox behind. The storeman down in Jefferson got his damned moneybox back with his money in it. Most of the money anyway, as far as I know.'

That stumped Joe Stiles. He stood in blending tree gloom studying what he could see of the cabin. Eventually, his face brightened. 'A cache,' he exclaimed and Twine put a dour look on Stiles.

'They're rangemen, worked for a big outfit down south. They'd have no reason to come up here; it's not cow country.' His voice rang with disgust. 'Joe, they come up here as posse riders; I'll lay you a bet they never come close to being up here before.'

Stiles didn't argue. Neither did he abandon his cache idea. He just did not mention it again. Instead he said, 'Go back, turn their horses loose, then we can walk 'em down.'

'An' what about Jane Bailey's horse out front of the house? To set 'em afoot up here that horse's got to be stampeded too.'

Joe Stiles faced his darker brother. 'Did you ever think positive in your life? You think like a damned In'ian, always the worst. Let's go.'

Twine accepted the tongue-lashing without much of a problem. He knew this much about the 'breed brother he'd lost track of many years earlier. Joe thought in a straight line and that for a fact was how Indians thought. Joe Stiles was more Indian than Twine Fourch ever had been or ever would be.

Locating the dozing saddle animals was no problem, but Twine didn't like the idea of just running them off. He told Joe to remove the saddles and bridles first.

When the animals discovered they were free they moved clear with a tentative trot swinging their heads. When they were satisfied, they went among the trees in a high lope heading southward downhill.

Twine and his brother went back where they could watch the house but several dozen yards south of where they had earlier watched.

Twine sat on a downed lightning-struck young fir tree. It bothered him that the renegades were still inside the cabin. To his knowledge there was no reason for them to stay in there so long. Joe had taken all the food.

Joe sagely nodded his head. 'Cache in there. I'll bet my life on it.'

Twine regarded his brother in disgust. He had told Joe those rangemen, like all their kind, avoided timbered country.

The possibility that Bailey and Carlile knew this area was very remote and Twine said so.

His brother, sitting on the ground with the Winchester against Twine's tree didn't turn his head from watching the cabin when he said, 'Then how come 'em to be there? Twine, there's a reason an' I'd bet they got a cache.'

Twine gently wagged his head. He had just learned something about the brother he had not known since childhood: Joe Stiles was as stubborn as a Missouri mule. When he got an idea in his head no argument under the sun would change his mind.

A skinny spindrift of smoke showed from the rock chimney and Twine said, 'They had grub with 'em. That's what they're doin' in there. Fixin' to eat; which reminds me, I haven't eaten since yestiddy.'

With the evidence of why the people were staying in the old cabin in plain sight, Joe's unshakeable conviction seemed less likely. He said, 'We got to get the sorrel horse.'

'It's a mare,' growled Twine, arising and dusting off. 'How do we do this?

It's out front of the house.'

When Joe Stiles answered, his words not only showed how different the brothers were but also that a man who existed off the land was canny. Stiles said, 'Spook the mare,' and also arose.

It was an obvious thing to say, but the problem remained: Jane Bailey's mount was out front of the cabin, anything it did would be noticed by the people inside.

Joe jerked his head and Twine followed until they came to a badly clawed old tree. Bears were not the only animals who tore trees. They did it to locate grubs and ants; other critters did it to sharpen their claws.

Stiles considered the tree which was slightly apart from other trees. He went close to the tree, yanked some ragged bark near the ground loose, passed it briefly in front of his face and tossed the large splinter aside. He did this three times before he found shredded bark that satisfied him. He held the armsized piece of fir-tree bark up to his brother's face and said, 'Cougar marked it.'

He used his uninjured arm, something Twine noticed briefly before stepping back. He understood the significance of the strong scent; as with all cats, mountain lions left urine specimens to mark either their territory or that they had passed this way.

Some very experienced riders have been unhorsed by mounts who pick up cougar scent. As a rule live-stock fear mountain lions above all carnivores, including bears.

Joe turned back, angling toward the stump area behind the cabin. Where he halted they had an excellent view of the back of the cabin. He was studying it when he said, 'Mind now, if something happens before I get down there, shoot and keep shootin'.'

Joe had to cross open ground. It was to his advantage that the old log house had no rear opening, neither a door nor a window. Another advantage was that Joe Stiles's moccasins made no sound.

He advanced, occasionally dropping behind a tree stump. Twine fisted his sidearm and scarcely breathed. If that thin spiral of smoke really meant the men inside were preparing a meal, Joe's stalk had a chance of success, but there were not many men who would attempt what Joe was doing.

He got to the rear log wall without incident. When he began creeping down the southerly wall Twine lost sight of him. He worried. As experienced as his brother was at stalking, the men inside that house were not game animals who would flee at the sight, scent or sound of a two-legged creature.

The smoke rose, there was no breeze and no noise. For Twine Fourch the waiting was agony. What eventually happened did so with noisy violence. The sorrel mare loudly snorted, sat violently back, broke her restraining reins and fled the way she had come travelling as fast as a 1200 pound horse could run.

The sudden eruption of noise inside the house was audible as far as Twine's point of advantage. He heard a door slammed open and was watching the south side of the cabin when someone's angry profanity coincided with Joe's appearance, running hard.

The loss of the sorrel mare was unlikely to genuinely upset Bailey and Carlile until the rat-faced man looked down, picked up the ragged scrap of tree bark, briefly examined it and said, 'Jess, there was no bark out here when we come up.'

Bailey ignored the wood in Carlile's hand as he stared at the other man and came to life about the time a winded 'breed met his brother and led the way further into the forest.

Neither of them heard Bailey say, 'Our horses!'

Carlile dropped the urine-impregnated piece of bark. 'Gawddamned cat,' he exclaimed, and his expression changed.

'There wasn't no bark before.' He continued to stare at Bailey who twisted to look around. Carlile spoke again. 'The son of a bitch is up here. She was lyin' when she said she hadn't seen him since down at the cow camp.'

Carlile started for the open door. Bailey stopped him midway. 'Maybe you're right, maybe it's that In'ian.'

Carlile had a fresh thought. 'I'm goin' to bring the horses down here.'

Bailey nodded about that. He also cautioned Carlile and the rat-faced man sounded contemptuous when he replied, 'You mind your sister, I'll be back directly.' Carlile paused before also saying, 'No reason to stay up here now, anyway.'

The forest watchers saw Carlile start away from the cabin and Joe led off back in the direction of the area where they had freed the renegades' horses.

Twine followed wondering about Jane Bailey. She would be safer in the cabin with her brother than she would have been if Bailey, instead of Carlile, had gone after their horses.

Joe was like a shadowy ghost. It helped that he knew every yard of this territory. The difficulty was that Carlile had less ground to cover than he and Twine. Carlile would discover that the horses were no longer where they should have been before he could be overtaken.

Nonetheless, Joe hastened. It was easier for him to cover ground in moccasins than it was for his brother wearing boots.

They heard Carlile before they saw him. He had discovered that the horses were gone and was standing over the saddles and bridles, possibly troubled over the fact that whoever had freed the horses had taken the time to make them really free.

Twine started forward. His brother flung out a stiff, restraining arm. They stood motionless until the rat-faced man slowly turned. It was possible that, as often happened under similar circumstances, he 'felt' the others.

Joe had been functioning by instinct so many years that he was watching Carlile from behind a huge old fir tree. Twine wasn't that savvy. He stood in deep shadows where he was discernible in vague outline. Carlile saw the outline and tensed as he stared. When Twine didn't move Carlile spoke in a fighting stance.

'Is that you, Fourch?'

Joe's answer came from hiding. 'No, it's me. Drop the gun an' don't move.'

The voice clearly hadn't come from the shadowed silhouette. Carlile hesitated then dropped his six-gun.

Joe told Twine to go over the renegade which Twine did and found an eight-inch boot knife and an under-and-over .44 derringer. He pocketed the pistol and threw the knife into some scraggly bushes.

Joe came into sight. Carlile looked at them both and exploded. 'I told that damned fool not to come back up here.'

'Why did he want to come?' Twine asked, and not only didn't expect an answer but got none.

Carlile stood glaring. 'What do you want?' he growled.

Twine spoke before his brother could. 'Bailey for murder an' you for robbery an' being Bailey's accessory . . . an' Jane Bailey.'

Carlile sneered, 'Far as I'm concerned you can have the woman. As for the rest of it, old possum-gut got his moneybox back an' we didn't steal it in the first place.'

Twine considered the rat-faced man. They had him, but that left the really dangerous one. 'Call Bailey to come out,' Twine said and Carlile's sneer deepened.

'Not on your damned life.'

Joe Stiles spoke up. 'Why did you come back here? Didn't you know Twine was after you?'

'We knew,' Carlile replied. 'We knew it before Jess's sister come along. We wasn't ready yet to leave.'

'Why?' Joe asked and got a snarling reply.

'Because we wasn't. We'd rode hard, hadn't ate well an' . . . '

'Now the real reason,' Twine interjected and Carlile glared.

'You deef? I just told you.'

Twine shook his head. 'After what happened up here, dumb as you two are, you aren't that dumb. Why?'

'Go to hell.'

Twine gestured with his drawn six-gun. 'Walk ahead of us to the cabin. Don't get clever. I've never back-shot a man in my life. If I got to do it now it won't bother me if it's you. *Walk!*'

Carlile didn't move, he glared from Twine to Joe Stiles and back. 'You can have the girl. She wasn't supposed to be up here. Jess was real surprised when she come. You can have her dead or alive. Dead if you try takin' us, alive if you tell me where your horses are an' let us leave.'

Twine said, 'Carlile . . . that's his sister.'

'Could be his mother, Constable. Won't bother me to shoot her.'

'It'll bother her brother,' Twine said, and again Carlile sneered.

'You don't know Jane Bailey. She's been trouble for him since she was whelped. She cussed him out for makin' their pa sell down until he's got precious little left to sell. He hates her guts. Me, well, if things was different . . .'

Twine repeated it. 'Walk ahead in front of us.'

Again Carlile sneered. 'You think Jess won't shoot. I've seen him shoot his way out before, mister. In our business don't matter whether someone needs a target or a sacrifice.'

Joe Stiles returned to his earlier question. 'Why the cabin? You had to figure Twine would dog you up here.'

'None of your damned business.'

Joe raised his pistol barrel until it was pointing at Carlile's soft parts. Carlile said, 'Go ahead. You pull that trigger'n Jess'll go where you can't ever find him.'

Twine holstered his weapon, stepped close and swung. Carlile went to his knees, shook his head like a gut-shot bear and without making any attempt to arise he said, 'You want to try that man to man?'

Twine grabbed cloth, hauled the rat-faced man to his feet and cocked a fist.

Carlile was sucking air, his middle hurt so much he thought he would heave. He raised an arm to deflect the blow he expected but which did not come as Twine shook him hard and released his grip. Carlile went down to all fours again.

Joe stepped in, leaned and put the cold blade of a wicked-looking skinning knife against Carlile's throat.

Carlile said, 'All right, I'll lead you down there,' and got awkwardly to his feet.

As they began to move, Twine told their captive to yell out that he couldn't find the horses. His idea was to catch Bailey when he came out of the cabin.

Carlile said, 'It won't work,' and kept on walking which he did with no spring in his step.

Joe interrupted part way along. He thought if they drew Bailey out he would see his partner being driven along and would start shooting. Joe Stiles had made his judgement on the basis of what he already knew about Jess Bailey as well as from what Carlile had said. He moved well to one side of his brother and Carlile, where he had a view of the south side of the cabin as well as the rear wall. He had no intention of giving Jess Bailey a chance. He had shot old Bean Severn out of hand; whatever his kin, particularly his sister in the cabin, thought of Jess Bailey, Joe Stiles was primed to kill him on sight.

Carlile stopped in the middle of the stump clearing and faced Twine Fourch. Twine said, 'Yell to him,' and Carlile shook his head.

'It ain't worth gettin' killed over . . . There's a cache down there.'

Joe Stiles snorted derisively. 'Damn liar . . . *walk!*'

Carlile did not heed Stiles, he addressed Twine. 'We hid it in there last spring. We robbed two stores over in Wheelerville an' stopped a stage on our way south. We spent two days scoutin' up this here Stone Mountain country an' found the old cabin. It was full of wood rats an' whatnot. Looked like nobody'd been there in years. We made the cache, rode on down to Jefferson, got hired on by Mr Morgan, figured to rob another store or a coach, an' when it happened that someone else done it, we hired on as possemen with the Jefferson storekeeper. Not to find his damned moneybox, to make damned sure no one found our cache.'

Twine was watching the house when he said, 'Where is the cache?'

'Behind that old fireplace. We took out rocks, hid the loot an' wedged the rocks back in place.'

'How much?' Twine asked, and the

answer surprised him.

'Seven pouches of raw gold an' six thousand in greenbacks.'

Joe stared. Twine's astonishment didn't show. He gestured with the pistol. '*Walk!*'

Carlile faced the cabin but didn't walk. 'He'll shoot me first,' he said, and stumbled when Joe gave him a hard punch from behind.

They reached the back log wall and stopped while Joe put his head to the wood, straightened up and softly said, 'They're arguin'.'

Carlile snorted. 'That's all they done since she rode up out front.'

Twine pushed Carlile and kept his left hand gripping shirt cloth as they went along the south wall. Twine stumbled over a half-submerged rock. Instantly the voices inside went silent. Someone wearing boots started toward the door. Carlile had been gone long enough to be now returning with the horses.

9

Beaten Men

Twine gave Carlile a rough push. As he stumbled into Bailey's view from the south side of the cabin Bailey said, 'You got 'em,' and when Carlile didn't answer, Bailey's scowl formed. He was about to speak when Joe Stiles appeared at the north corner of the house with a cocked six-gun and said, 'Drop it!'

Bailey seemed turned to stone. Twine was out of sight along the south wall several feet behind Carlile. He heard his brother speak and waited for the sound of Bailey's sidearm being dropped. Instead what he heard sounded like splitting wood with a dull axe as Jane Bailey struck her brother hard enough to knock him down with a dry old scantling of fir wood.

Bailey was struggling for breath as he tried to arise. The impact hadn't only knocked Bailey to the ground, it had loosened his grip on the six-gun. It slid to within two or three feet of Carlile who seemed too stunned to speak.

Twine stepped into sight, moved without haste to plant a boot atop Bailey's six-gun.

Joe Stiles hadn't moved. All of them except the leggy woman in the doorway stood rooted. Jess Bailey scrabbled in the dirt sucking air. The blow had caught him high in the back, its force had nearly knocked the wind out of him.

Twine looked at the girl, at her writhing brother and was still standing with one foot on Bailey's pistol when Joe approached, nodded to the girl, caught hold of Bailey from behind and yanked him to his feet. Bailey leaned forward fighting for breath.

Twine asked Jane Bailey if she had been hurt and got a dry answer. 'He's still my brother.'

They had to help Bailey into the cabin where there was nothing to sit on. They lowered him to the floor where Joe watched him like a hawk while Twine gruffly thanked Jane Bailey, and detracted from whatever pleasure she might have derived from that statement by also saying, 'You're worse'n a leech.'

For Carlile, for whatever might have been, a period of loafing was shattered. He went over by the fireplace and leaned there watching his partner. When Bailey could straighten up and was putting a murderous stare on his sister, Carlile said, 'Jess, I told you one of them caves up yonder would be better.'

Bailey put his sulphurous look on his partner. 'You said a lot of things, you damned imbecile.'

Twine jerked his head for Carlile to follow and left the cabin. He said, 'Show me,' and Carlile obeyed.

On the side of the cabin where someone had painstakingly created a rock chimney Carlile spread the fingers of one hand, crab-walked them and stopped as he said, 'Here,' and as Twine considered what was nearly a perfect replacement of mud and stone Carlile also said, 'All right, I told you an' I showed you. Now it's your turn. Stay here while I get a-horseback and leave.'

Twine's response was curt. 'Not on my horse,' and gestured. 'Take the rocks out.'

Carlile had to strain, not only had the stones been replaced, they had been hammered to fit each niche. Carlile growled that he needed something besides his hands and Twine's response was, 'Dig, you son of a bitch!'

When two of the boulders were levered loose and fell, removing the others was easier. When the hole was exposed Twine pushed Carlile aside and groped. He brought forth four buckskin pouches and someone's blue bandanna tied into a large bundle. The sacks were small but heavy. The bandanna was less weighty.

Carlile frowned. 'There's more sacks. Three more.'

He was right. The reason Twine hadn't located them before was because they had slid deeper down the hole. Twine shoved his left arm in up to his shoulder, felt buckskin and lifted out three more heavy little pouches.

Carlile said, 'Mister, if you got a lick of sense you'n me'll get a-horseback and keep riding. There's enough gold and greenbacks to divvy up an' both of us can live right well for a long time.'

Twine seemed not to have heard. He gestured with his handgun. 'Pick it up an' go inside.'

As Carlile was leaning to obey he said, 'You're a damned fool 'breed. You won't see this much loot again if you live to a hunnert.'

'Shut up and walk!'

When Carlile appeared in the cabin where burned-down candles made light, Jess Bailey got to his feet glaring. Carlile faced him. 'You try it, Jess, with a gun in your back.'

Jane was puttering at the fireplace. Her reward was a tongue of flames which she carefully fed before arising to lean on the slat she had struck her brother with.

She was looking at Twine when she said, 'That's why they came up here?' and when Twine brusquely nodded she addressed her brother. 'You couldn't even make it as an outlaw. I told Pa a couple of years back he'd ought to forget he had a son.'

Bailey could not help but to have heard but his attention was on the seven pouches and the blue bandanna.

Joe Stiles said, 'That's more nuggets than I've dug an' panned in ten years.'

Jane Bailey brought a limp length of warm jerky to Twine, who took it and began chewing.

It was late. He wouldn't risk taking the outlaws down to Jefferson in the dark. Joe's idea was to tie them until daylight then herd them southward on foot.

Twine was agreeable; he was too tired

to do anything else, but he watched Jane Bailey when she helped his brother lash the wrists and ankles of her brother and John Carlile.

He left Joe to watch the others, went to find his horse, bring it to the corral and unlash his bedroll from behind the cantle.

When he returned to the house it was almost too warm. His brother was sitting on the floor, Winchester across his lap, snoring like a shoat caught under a gate.

Jane was not only awake, she was feeding the fire and when Twine appeared he said, 'It's already as hot in here as the hubs of hell,' she arose, went over where the old woman's cot had been and hunkered without taking her eyes off Twine.

He considered Joe. If both of them slept . . . He looked at the girl. 'Any more sticks of that jerky?'

She brought him two more limp, warm pieces and kept one for herself. She looked at him. 'Lie down, you look plumb tuckered.'

He was 'plumb tuckered' but he chewed, said nothing and when he looked at her she read his mind.

'I wouldn't turn them loose if my life depended on it.'

He continued to regard her and chew. She walked back where the cot had been and sat down. 'Mr Fourch, I've seen some pig-stubborn men in my life but you take the prize. Why would I turn them loose?'

He didn't answer. He turned his back to her, shed his hat, scuffed out of his boots and went down, still with his back to her and his six-gun in his right fist.

Everyone had limits. Twine Fourch had pushed beyond his limits. Tough as rawhide or not, moments before he dozed off he speculated on the next day, decided it could take care of itself and slept like the dead.

What awakened him was someone angrily cursing. He listened, gun in hand. The fire was down to coals, the burned-down candles were wavering in the last of their wax.

Jess Bailey was swearing at his sister. She sat against the far wall barely visible in the failing light. She had a six-gun fisted in her lap. When her brother had to pause for breath she said, 'You broke Pa's heart even more'n when Ma ran off. You're worthless, Jess. I've known it since we were kids.'

His answer was direct. 'You see them pouches an' that handkerchief stuffed with greenbacks? You set me loose, I'll take half the loot, you can have the rest. I'll take a horse an' as Gawd's my witness neither you nor Pa'll ever see me again.'

The girl was poised to speak when Twine sat up and said, 'Your pa'll never see you again anyway, Bailey. Down in Jefferson folks thought kindly of that old man you killed. Lie back an' go to sleep!'

Bailey had reason not to sleep, the impaired circulation in his arms wouldn't let him.

He did not lie back down either, he glared at Twine. 'You damned 'breed, if I was loose I'd scalp you alive.'

A grumbling voice came out of the flickering light. 'Shut up, you two argue after sun-up.'

Other than listening to what Carlile had to say none of the others heeded him.

For a while there was quiet. Twine was ready to lie back when Bailey spoke again, his voice different.

'Half to you an' the loan of your horse, Constable. It's more'n you'll make workin' for wages in ten years.' Bailey paused briefly. 'I'll throw in my sister. She's real ripe, Mr Fourch.'

Neither Jane nor Twine had expected that last remark. It embarrassed them both so much after it was said the cabin was as silent as a grave.

Until Bailey showed a wolfish smile in the poor light and spoke again. 'I've seen worse an' so have you. If you want to keep her for a pet, she's a tolerable good cook an' can shoe a horse with the best of 'em.'

Bailey might have had more inducements to offer, but his sister sprang up and hurled the six-gun as hard as she could. Her brother sucked back. The gun struck Joe Stiles alongside the head. He didn't move.

Twine kicked out of his bedroll, crossed swiftly to intercept Jane. He made it, but she aimed a furious kick at her brother and this time she didn't miss. Jess Bailey let go with a pained squawk and doubled over.

She was a handful even for Twine Fourch. She was not only tall and muscular without an ounce of spare flesh, she could strike faster than a rattlesnake.

Twine absorbed the first blow and sidestepped to avoid the next one. She stood poised and he waited to grab her arm. Very slowly she came down from the peak of her anger.

She said, 'I'll kill him!'

Twine didn't dispute that possibility,

but he said, 'Not here,' and pushed her away.

One inhabitant of the cabin slept through everything, his cadenced snores never missing a beat. Twine considered his brother, sleeping like a log on a hardpan floor, shrugged and returned to his blankets. Joe had probably rarely slept any other way. Danged Indian!

When dawn arrived, Twine had both arms under his head as he watched the candles die and new-day light taking their place.

He stamped into his boots, went outside to the corral to fork some of that dust and spiderweb-infested hay and went to the creek to wash. He heard her, but when he looked around she was not in sight. He finished at the creek and was drying off when she came from the south. She had been looking for her sorrel mare. When he said the animal was most likely halfway home by now, she shook her head. 'I raised her from a filly. I've turned her out dozens of times and she follows me back to the house.'

'How's your brother an' his friend?'

'Your brother's watching them. Twine . . . ?'

'Yes'm.'

'My brother's a filthy-mouthed, no-good renegade.'

He slightly smiled as he stowed the wiping bandanna away. 'Any of that jerky left, ma'am?'

She flared at him. 'You're thicker'n a post. My name's Jane, not ma'am.'

He accepted that calmly. 'I'm hungry, Jane.'

When they reached the cabin, Joe Stiles was nursing a lump on the side of his head and wearily looked at them. 'I thought you'n her was gone. Someone hit me on the head. It wasn't them two.'

Jane explained that she had missed her brother and the thrown gun had struck Joe Stiles. He looked long at her before heading for the door, shouldering Jane and his brother roughly aside as he did so.

Bailey said he was hungry and thirsty. Twine left his sister to worry about that while he hoisted Carlile against the wall, freed his arms. He wanted to know where the money and gold had come from. All Carlile could tell him was that he and Jess Bailey had taken it from the stage they robbed and Twine looked stonily at him. 'You said somethin' about robbin' a store.'

Carlile nodded. 'Yeah. The general store up north.'

'What other robberies did you two commit?'

Carlile avoided answering as Jane brought two more of those heated and limp sticks of jerky to Twine. Carlile looked up at her. 'You got some for me?'

She turned her back and walked over to her brother. As they looked at each other he said, 'You double-crossin' damned . . . '

The slap sounded almost like a pistol shot. Bailey almost went over sideways. Twine went over there, took her by the arm and led her toward the fireplace. As he released her he said, 'Leave 'em be.'

She faced away from him without speaking. He returned to Carlile, hunkered and resumed his questioning.

There had been a killing up north. As Carlile talked he avoided looking at Jess Bailey. 'We was ridin' wore-down horses, come over a hill an' saw three rangemen leave a ranch yard. We rode there. A woman seen us go into the barn and come after us with a shotgun. Jess knocked her down and kicked the shotgun away. He didn't see the kid, he was fixin' to lead a fresh horse out of a stall. I seen him come sneakin' around the front barn opening. He had a six-shooter and was fixin' to cock it when I yelled. Jess spun and shot twice. The first one missed but the second one dropped the kid in his tracks. The slug hit him dead centre in the brisket.'

Twine turned. 'Is that true, Bailey?'

Jane's brother reddened. 'No! John

shot the kid. I didn't even see him.'

Carlile stared at Bailey without saying a word.

Twine stood up facing the girl. 'Go see if your mare came back. It's time to head down out of here.'

Jane left the cabin, almost bumped into Joe who was returning. She said, 'I'm sorry.'

Joe looked steadily at her, shoved past and entered the house. He not only had a lump, he had a headache all the way down to his feet.

As he entered he faced his brother. 'Where's she goin'?'

'To find her mare.'

'The mare's behind the corral nosin' your horse over the rocks.' Joe eyed the prisoners. 'You goin' to take 'em down to Jefferson?'

'Yes. You want to come along?'

'No! Not if my life depended on it. All I want is to soak my head in the creek. That danged woman. I never heard of one that could shoot straight an' that goes for throwin' things.' He eyed the prisoners again. 'Put ropes around their necks. If they run all you got to do is take dallies and set up your horse. It'll snap their necks like a twig.'

Jane returned beaming, she had found her sorrel mare.

Twine unshipped his holstered Colt as he told her to untie their ankles. As she was doing this he told Carlile and Bailey he'd do as Joe suggested. If they tried escaping he'd break their necks.

Carlile said nothing but Jane's brother did. 'I got a cache, Constable. Four thousand dollars' worth.'

Carlile interrupted with a derisive snort. Twine looked at him and the rat-faced man said, 'He don't have no cache an' he don't have no four thousand dollars.'

Twine gestured with his six-gun. 'On your feet.'

They obeyed without looking at each other, but there was no mistaking Bailey's expression, if he got the chance he would kill Twine and his sister, but first he would kill John Carlile.

Joe lingered to help get the horses ready. The last thing he did was place ropes around two necks and make sure they had loose-fitting slip knots.

As Twine and Jane got mounted Joe stood to one side looking as fierce toward the mounted riders as at their prisoners. He did not wish them a safe trip, in fact he didn't even raise his hand in the customary parting salute and, as they passed from sight among the southward timber, he turned and struck out northward in the direction of his camp outside the rocked-up grave of his mother.

Before the riders and their captives reached level ground, Jess Bailey developed a limp from stepping on a rock that had spun sideways from under his foot. He told Twine his ankle was either sprained or broken. If that statement was supposed to elicit anxiety or concern it did neither. Twine told Bailey to pick up a stick and use it as a cane and not to stop walking.

Carlile malevolently grinned at Bailey to whom he attributed his own difficulty.

No one spoke until shortly before they left the uplands for flat country, down where the sun shone with uninterrupted force.

Bailey not only stumbled and panted but croaked for water. Neither Jane nor Twine carried canteens. Twine told him to angle easterly, there was a creek over yonder and Jane shook her head at Twine. She knew her brother; when they reached a place where they could stop, water or no water, he was desperate; he knew the finality of what lay ahead.

She said nothing, but rode behind her brother with the rope to Carlile loosely looped around her saddlehorn.

There was a creek, but they didn't reach it until the sun was slanting away from its meridian.

Jess Bailey threw himself down and drank. Carlile drank, too, with a distance between himself and Jess Bailey of about thirty feet.

Twine wagged his head the way Jane's brother gulped water down. Too much and he would not only throw it up but would be sick as a dog. Between the wrenched ankle and overloading with water on an empty stomach . . . It was still a good five miles to Jefferson. Jane told her brother to stop drinking. He did not look around where she was standing beside her sorrel mare but he dug deeply into creek-side mud with both hands. He hadn't really been drinking; at first, yes. Later he kept his face in water but didn't drink.

Carlile said something to Twine who turned to answer. A deer fly landed on the forehead of the sorrel mare. Jane twisted raising her hand.

Jess Bailey came upright in one smooth movement, jumped at Twine and hurled the mud. Part of it struck Twine's face. Instinctively he threw up a hand for protection, unable to see.

10

A Dead Man

John Carlile remained immobile at the creek. His partner swung Twine half around groping for his holstered sidearm.

Jane had been poised to kill the deer fly with her right hand. The distance was too great for her to use her Colt.

She turned facing her brother. He had Twine's gun pushed hard into Twine's back over the kidneys. Twine lowered his right hand to the empty holster and continued to wipe his face with the other hand.

Jane didn't raise her voice when she said, 'Jess, don't do this.'

His reply was to cock Twine's six-gun and glare. She spoke again. 'Jess! Listen to me. Don't . . . '

He snarled. 'Double-crossin' bitch. It

didn't mean nothin' to you that we're blood kin. I'd ought to shoot you.'

From the creek Carlile spoke harshly. 'Take the horses an' let's get away from here.'

Bailey's reaction stunned his sister and Twine Fourch. Bailey turned slightly, aimed low and fired. The impact knocked Carlile part way into the creek where diluted reddish water ran.

Twine's eyes were watering but he could see. He saw Jane jump clear of her mare and lunge for her pistol.

She was an excellent pistol shot but with no reason to practise speed, did not make a fast draw, nor would it have made much difference. The fastest gun on earth can't beat another gun already up and aimed.

Twine jerked his shoulders as Bailey shot. The bullet severed one rein of the sorrel mare who shied yanking the remaining rein from Jane's left hand.

Bailey screamed a curse, violently

punched the gun deeper into Twine's back until the pain was almost unbearable.

Twine cried out and wrenched violently away then whirled back and kicked as hard as he could. He had tried to hit Bailey's gun hand or his arm. He missed and Jess Bailey fired his third shot as Twine was falling. No moving target, a voluntary or involuntary one, is desirable. Bailey was wild-eyed and frantic. He missed.

His sister had time to draw and fire. She, too, had hurried. The bullet struck Carlile's corpse which only sluggishly moved under impact.

Twine rolled up to his feet as Bailey twisted toward him. Jane fired her second shot, this time from a poised position. Her brother's bullet ploughed earth in front of Twine as he was falling.

The entire episode required less than two minutes.

Twine dug out his bandanna, wiped his eyes, dropped the bandanna and went to toe Jess Bailey over on to his back. He snarled like a wolf which Twine ignored to look for the wound. He found it when he rolled Bailey on to his stomach. The entire lower portion of his shirt was soaked with blood.

Twine knelt for a closer inspection. When he straightened up Jane was getting on her mare. He called to her. He needed help to stop the bleeding. She mounted, rode southward at a walk without speaking or looking back.

Bailey huskily said, 'Let her go. It don't matter how far she rides she'll remember. Let her go.'

Twine tore the soggy shirt to make a bandage that went completely around Bailey. When it was tight he forced his bandanna inside to further impede the bleeding.

Bailey vomited pure water. Twine had to drag him clear. From where Twine stopped, Bailey could see John Carlile soggily rising and falling with the water. He made no attempt to speak but his expression showed bitter satisfaction.

Twine had a long walk ahead holding Bailey in the saddle. Dusk was approaching. His personal feeling was that Bailey would not survive the trip; it didn't bother him.

He would send someone back for Carlile, but he would deliver Jess Bailey in Jefferson sitting the saddle or tied across it.

Bailey wasn't always coherent. Once he mumbled something about that damned kid should've shot, he had the drop. Another time he said John Carlile was a whining bastard.

Twine was not accustomed to long walks and it seemed he would never see rooftops or lamplight. His horse adjusted to the slower pace of its owner, made no attempt to lean when the man on its back sagged. Twine had to do that. If Bailey fell, Twine wasn't sure he could ever get him back up in the saddle.

His back hurt, every step he took

reminded him that he had been jammed hard in the unprotected portion of his back.

They had covered something like two miles with night closing around them when Twine thought he heard sounds in the direction of Jefferson, but since they came and went he attributed the incident to mild hallucinations.

He used the saddle thongs to tie Bailey around the middle. They were barely long enough.

As he walked, thoughts flooded in. The most prominent one was remembering the sight of Bailey's sister leaving the creek at a dead walk, erect in the saddle as though nothing had happened back yonder.

He also remembered her expression of disapproval when he had said they would stop at the creek. His lips pulled up in a bitter small smile. She had been right, they shouldn't have stopped.

A vagrant thought told him the reason she had ridden off the way she had was because she had been monumentally disgusted with Twine for stopping at the creek when he had to know every step closer to town they got her brother's desperation would increase.

His assumption was wrong, but he believed it. Regardless of how little she cared for her brother and regardless that he had killed two people in cold blood, one a child, Jess Bailey was still her brother. Her blood kin.

She had demonstrated her blood-loyalty several times — and she had shot him.

Twine had a grouping of light in sight when the noise he thought he had imagined a mile or so back, firmed up in the night. It was a light dray wagon.

A man hailed him. Twine stopped and leaned on his horse. The driver was Will Morgan who had employed Bailey and Carlile. Morgan was, aside from being a successful stockman, a greying individual who was neither easily angered nor shocked. Beside him on the spring seat was Jane Bailey, her face white in the moonlight.

Morgan handed the lines to Jane, climbed down, looked long at Jess Bailey, made a little clucking sound and lifted him from the saddle, took him to the tailgate of the light wagon and placed him gently atop some vile-smelling fresh cow hides.

Jane did not get down. She sat up there ignoring everything but Twine Fourch. When Morgan settled the tailgate chain he dried both hands on a white bandanna and stood briefly regarding Twine.

He said, 'You better ride back with us. I'll tie your horse to the tailgate.'

Twine shook his head as he said, 'If you got a canteen . . . '

Morgan fished under the seat, found the canteen and handed it over. Twine raised it, swallowed slowly looking straight at Jane Bailey. When he handed the canteen back he told her for the second time that he was hungry.

She didn't smile, she nodded her

head. 'I'll ride your horse back,' she said, and climbed down to the ground.

As Twine handed her the reins she very softly said, 'The medical man is waiting. How is he?'

Twine replied bluntly, 'I'm surprised he hung on this long.'

As he was climbing to the wagon seat Bailey loudly muttered something indistinguishable and Morgan said, 'Out of his head', as he made a wide turn, talked up the horse and headed for town.

Jane rode on the right side of the wagon bed. If her brother recognized her or even knew a rider was there he gave no indication of it.

Twine sagged, head down and slept. From time to time the cowman looked over. He had known the Jefferson township lawman for years. They had little in common, therefore they had never become close friends, but Will Morgan had heard enough over the years to base respect upon. But, right now in watery moonlight, Twine

Fourch, unshaven, shaggy-headed in soiled clothing looked like a desperado, not a lawman.

By the time they reached Jefferson store fronts were locked and dark. There were infrequent lights among houses. In front of the livery barn a pair of carriage lamps shone upon a pair of greying men sitting loosely on an ancient wooden bench.

At the sound of the wagon, the only moving object the full length of Jefferson's roadway, they both arose peering northward. The liveryman said, 'It'll be them.'

His companion said nothing. He was a stocky individual with a respectable paunch, a head of unruly curly greying hair. His air was of a man accustomed to whatever life put in front of him. His name was Alvin Kimmel; he was a physician who, on his way north, had been waylaid in Jefferson by townsmen who somehow knew his services would shortly be needed. In fact, they had gone to the trouble of making a room ready in the empty parsonage behind Jefferson's Methodist Church.

When Morgan made a wide sweep before entering the barn's runway the liveryman began making clucking noises and Twine abruptly awakened. Morgan looked enquiringly at him. Twine ignored that, climbed down and watched Jane dismount near the tailgate.

Morgan had loaded Jess Bailey by himself. The unloading required Twine, the physician and the liveryman who continued to cluck. Jess Bailey, even in poor light, looked like someone who had been butchering cattle.

They got him up to the parsonage about the time several townsmen came through the spindle doors of the only lighted business establishment, the saloon.

They watched three men carrying a fourth one northward trailed by a long-legged woman. One of them said, 'That'll be Twine Fourch got himself shot.'

Another customer of the saloon disagreed. 'That's Twine on the lee side, watch for light. It's him.'

'Then who's the feller they're carryin'?'

There was no answer to that but a large unkempt, unshaven man said, 'Let's go find out.'

They reached the opposite plankwalk before Twine heard and saw them. He didn't miss a step when he told them to mind their own damned business. They stopped in silence before eventually crossing back over to the saloon where they made some outlandish guesses which the barman didn't heed; late evening business hadn't been so good in months.

The parsonage smelled musty although it had been swept and dusted. After Jess Bailey was put on a long table and lamps were brought, the doctor shed his coat, peeled up his sleeves and went to work. He was no different from most frontier medicine men, he carried in his little satchel bandaging cloth, disinfectant, laudanum, as well as cutting and stitching implements.

Jane stood by a window out of the way. When Twine looked at her she seemed to be supporting herself against the sill of the window.

He took her by the arm, closed the door after them and guided her out into the cold air. There was a bench with a slatted back rest. He eased her down, drew several deep breaths then said, 'It couldn't be helped.'

She replied in a leaden voice. 'How do I tell Pa? Jess was his pride and joy. Rotten as Pa eventually knew he was, he never missed a chance to tell how good a roper an' reinsman his Jess-boy was. My ma ran off with a travelling man. That nearly killed Pa. Now this . . . '

Twine had no answers; he eased down beside her on the bench looking almost stoically at stars that seemed to flicker and water.

'Twine . . . ?'

'Yes'm.'

'Are you still hungry?'

'Yes'm.'

'I have a close friend. We could go wake her up and make you a meal.'

He pushed out scuffed boots and regarded them. 'Jane-girl, I'm hungry for a fact . . . I lost a mother I never knew an' a brother I don't have anythin' in common with. I guess I feel a little like you do right now. I'm hungry, but I'm not sure I could eat.'

They sat in silence for a long time and would probably have remained that way longer if the doctor hadn't come out to the porch in shirtsleeves.

He said, 'The wound won't kill him but the loss of blood very well could.'

Jane had a question. 'When will you know?'

The doctor offered an oblique reply. 'Miss Bailey, I'm due in Willows by morning. Willows is eighty miles from here. It's an emergency. I can't even guess how long his recovery will take if he recovers at all . . . I have to be on the dawn stage north . . . It'll be up to whoever takes care of him.'

The physician paused. 'Don't expect too much from the best care you can give him.'

The doctor returned to his patient leaving Jane and Twine as still and silent as before, until she finally said, 'Pa'll have to be told.'

Twine remained silent. There was little doubt about what she had said, but when he shifted on the bench she came back from her reverie and stood up. 'Come along; we'll get you fed.'

They walked in silence until she turned in at a dark small cottage and knocked on the door as she spoke. 'Her name is Lucille Emory. She's a railroad widow.'

When the door opened, Lucille Emory, with a lighted lamp backgrounding her, looked younger than her seventy years. She was wrapped in a thick bathrobe which she held close.

Jane explained; the elderly woman stepped aside for them to enter and without a word picked up the lamp and went directly to the kitchen. She knew something about hungry men but this was the first time she had one appear on her doorstep in the middle of the night.

She didn't ask questions, she didn't have to; Jane talked without interruption until the meal was ready and they awakened Twine sitting asleep at the kitchen table.

The elderly widow knew who Twine was. They had never officially nor socially met but Lucille Emory had come to Jefferson a year or two before Twine had; she had seen him dozens of times.

But right now he hardly resembled the town constable she knew by sight.

She did a surprising thing for a 70-year-old widow woman, she produced a three-quarters-full bottle of whiskey and put it and a glass in front of the constable.

He smiled and went back to eating. He did not touch the bottle, not even after he had arisen from the table with pleats out of his stomach.

He thanked the widow woman, offered to pay and when she stiffened at that suggestion he said, 'As fine a meal as I've ever eaten,' and the stiffness left her. She cocked her head a little. 'My husband's razor and shaving mug are on the back porch, Constable.'

He wavered. What he really wanted and needed more than being presentable was to sleep the clock around. He might have mentioned this if the widow woman hadn't led him to the back porch with its wash bowl, soap and razor lying atop a clean towel and smiled.

Jane said, 'I'll help with the dishes,' and they left him alone.

He didn't shave. He sat on a wall bench and fell asleep. When they looked in on him later Lucille Emory said, 'Fetch the quilt from the parlour, Jane. He can't be comfortable setting like that but at least he'll be warm.'

After Jane left, the widow woman gave her head a slight wag and blew out a big sigh. It was like old times except that when her husband had fallen asleep like this it was because he had imbibed too much.

When Twine awakened, the house was chilly and quiet. He stoked up a fire in the cook stove, drank coffee and left the house.

Dawn was breaking. He went down to look after his horse and the liveryman, who was pitching feed, answered his question succinctly.

'She went out of here some time last night. The horse was here when I left. When I come up this morning it was gone an' my night man didn't know it until I showed him the empty stall.' The liveryman leaned on his pitchfork as he said, 'Constable, I got no idea how well you know them Baileys but they're a clanny bunch. I've heard the talk about Jess. If I had to guess I'd say she rode to the ranch to tell old Wayne his boy's in bad shape in town.'

Twine went to the eatery where he was greeted with reserve by other early morning diners as well as the caféman who served Twine breakfast without speaking.

He went up to the corralyard where Justin Abbot was friendly. He had more reason to be. He at least had been involved up at Stone Mountain. He told Twine the medicine man had left Jefferson by the dawn's northbound. He also told him the talk around town was that Twine had shot Jess Bailey, an erroneous notion Twine did not bother correcting.

At his jailhouse, he fired up the stove, considered the pile of correspondence on his table and sat down, kicked back and stared at the opposite wall.

If old Wayne Bailey should come to town, there would be a meeting between them as a matter of course. He scratched his unshaven face and speculated whether Jane had told her father who had shot her brother. She could avoid the inevitable and enduring change of heart the old man would have toward his daughter by not telling the truth. He also speculated that if she avoided the truth and Wayne Bailey believed Twine had shot his son it wouldn't make much difference. They had only met once.

The blacksmith's helper to whom Twine had given his job came in and tossed Twine's extra badge on the desk as he said, 'Mr Fourch, except for drunks nothin' much happened but I wouldn't have your job for a lot of money.'

After the younger man departed, Twine arose to go stand at the little barred roadway window thinking his temporary replacement had a point.

He had little time to dwell on this because Calvin Lott arrived wearing his merchant's apron and beaming.

'I told folks you'd be after them two bastards if it took the rest of your life. Twine, as a councilman I'm goin' to recommend you for better pay.'

Twine considered the older man; he had knocked Lott down at the cabin and was sure Lott hadn't forgotten.

He said, 'Was the full three thousand in the box?'

'Exceptin' ten dollars it was. I owe you, boy. The whole town owes you.'

After the storekeeper left, Twine went down to rig out his horse and leave town with the sun on his back riding westerly in the direction of the Bailey ranch.

11

Something Else

The yard was empty and the house sent forth an aura of something Twine couldn't define as he entered the yard. Except for an old cow with horn maggots, shaking her head, there was no movement.

He tied up at the tie rack in front of the house. It wasn't possible in most ranch yards for someone to enter a yard and not be seen.

As Twine raised a fist to rattle the door it was yanked open, not by Jane but by her darkly pretty sister whose eyes were moist. She offered no greeting, simply stepped aside for him to enter.

The house was chilly. No one had built a fire. The dark girl gestured for Twine to be seated. He obeyed and removed his hat.

That Jane's sister was upset was obvious, coupled to that was the unnatural quiet. He fidgeted, finally went to stand by the front window. He could see the old cow occasionally shaking her head. As far as he could see she had both horns so the flies had to have entered by some other route to lay the eggs from which maggots hatched and seriously upset cows.

He was watching the cow wondering why someone hadn't sidelined it to the corral and put chloroform-soaked cotton into the horn when Jane appeared soundlessly and said, 'I knew you'd come,' and gave him no opportunity to speak. She jerked her head for him to follow, left the house and led the way to the old log barn. The abrupt change from bright sunlight to dark barn light made him pause in the wide doorway.

When she stopped, her back was to Twine. As his indoor vision improved she said, 'Help me,' and started forward.

Twine only saw why she had said that when he looked up. Her father was hanging from an overhead baulk. His eyes were closed, his lips, like the rest of his face, were putty grey.

Twine moved as Jane opened a clasp knife to cut the taut rope. Twine caught the body and lowered it to the ground. Until he had done this he hadn't said a word. Now he looked at her.

'When, Jane?'

'Sometime in the night. My sister found him. When I rode in she was crying on the porch.'

Twine stood looking down. The old man's face didn't show any of that peaceful serenity it was said came to the features of the dead. He looked bitter.

Twine spoke without looking up. 'Why? If you didn't get here until this morning, then he didn't know.'

Jane contradicted him. 'He knew. The Kingmans, who adjoin us, returned from town yesterday and told him Jess was dying, that the constable had shot him.'

She abruptly sat on the ground beside her father and tears flowed.

Twine returned to the sunlight. There was no sign of Jane's sister. The only sound was of that old cow being driven to distraction by maggots. The sound put his nerves on edge. He stepped back into the barn.

'If I'd come home last night I could have told him Jess was in good hands . . . Twine? He reached his limit. He never recovered from my mother running off, and Jess, well, he did his best to put on a good face to folks about him.'

Twine knew she was strong so when she jumped up and threw herself into his arms he was completely unprepared, but he responded instinctively by putting his arms around her.

Looking ahead and downward he saw her father lying there. He led her out the rear of the barn where the old cow stopped rattling her horns at the sight of them. She went to the stone trough and drank.

Twine didn't remember where he had lost his bandanna but it was not in his pocket so he looked for something for Jane to wipe her eyes with and when he looked back she had produced her own cloth; it was a white handkerchief not a bandanna.

She had a brief bout of hiccups, went to the trough to splash water in her face. When she straightened up she and the old cow looked straight at each other before Jane spoke absently.

'There's a brown bottle on a shelf in the harness room. If you'll sideline her I'll pour some in.'

Twine went after the brown bottle. When he returned, Jane was inside the corral, she was at one end, the old cow was at the other. She handed Twine a lass rope from the saddle pole in the barn. He shook out a loop and looked at her, but she was sidling along the corral poles toward the cow. He knew what he was supposed to do, he had seen it done many times, but he had cowboyed only briefly and that had been years back.

She would spook the old girl past him on the opposite side of the corral. She was too distant for him to tell her he hadn't used a lariat in years, and even back then he hadn't been very good at roping.

She got the cow untracked. It saw Twine up ahead and Jane in back. From many calving times she knew what was impending, but with no recourse she began gingerly advancing.

Corral roping is a science; ordinarily, critters walk up to a point then break over into a wild run. Seasoned ropers wait for the run. Twine shook out a loop. The cow saw him do that and bunched to charge past, but only ran fifteen or twenty feet then jammed down to a stiff-legged halt at the moment he hurled the loop. It fell in front of the cow where she was supposed to be but wasn't.

If Jane had been a man she would

have cursed with feeling. Because she wasn't a man, she simply walked up and took the rope from Twine. All she said was, 'Get behind her, keep her moving.'

The result of this change proved satisfactory to all but the old cow. When the rope settled and tightened she threw a fit.

Twine ran forward to lend his weight to Jane's weight.

Tame animals like milk cows rarely move when a rope tightens. This old girl was range born and bred. She did everything but charge the ropers. She raised dust, bawled and slobbered.

Twine took the turk's-head end of the lass, got around the cow, got the rope through between stringers and when she fought he took up slack until she was hard against the stringers with her head twisted.

Jane approached with the bottle and Twine kept the rope taut and held his breath. The old girl had hooks close to three feet long on each side.

Jane took the slack from Twine, went past the cow's head, looped it through stringers and threw all her weight until it was almost as tight as a fiddle string. She made the tag-end fast. The cow could struggle but she couldn't get free.

Twine was fascinated at the way Jane went up to the near side horn, looked for an opening, found none, climbed to the topmost corral stringer on the opposite side, found the hole and poured chloroform in.

The old cow fought like a tiger, barely missed hooking Jane as she climbed down on the outside of the corral and called to Twine she would in-tie her end and for him to let there be slack.

When the cow discovered she was free she went charging toward the far end of the corral head high and shaking.

They saw the ball of wet maggots soar and land. Jane said, 'She'll shake loose of the noose,' and went to the trough to wash her hands.

When Twine came up she looked around. 'Didn't you ever do roping?'

'When I was young, but not much then an' I never was good at it.'

The old cow had done more than get rid of her maggots she had provided a needed diversion for the two-legged things.

Jane dried her hands as she said, 'You're hungry.'

While he was washing he didn't speak so she said, 'Now we got the cow doctored I think you need worming.'

He spoke while shaking off water. 'Worming?'

'You're always hungry.'

Neither of them smiled but neither did they re-enter the barn, they went strolling northward until they ran out of outbuildings before Jane spoke again. 'Will you help me?'

He nodded. It required no prescience to know what she was talking about; would he help her bury her father.

A horseman appeared far to the east.

They stopped to watch, neither of them could recognize him at that distance but consistent with Jane Bailey's present frame of mind she eventually said, 'Jess's dead,' and resumed walking, this time in the direction of the house.

Twine followed in dogged silence. When Jane opened the door for him to enter he shook his head and asked a one-word question.

'Where?'

Her reply was softly said, 'Under that tree beyond the rear of the barn,' and went inside. As she was closing the door, Twine went as far as the bottom stair-step and halted to watch the oncoming rider who was not hurrying. He had the same premonition Jane'd had.

He continued to the barn, found a stained wagon canvas and rolled Wayne Bailey in it. Then he searched for digging tools after dragging the dead man to a secluded, dark place.

The rider entered the yard at a walk, angled toward the tie pole out front of the barn, saw Twine inside and hailed him. It was Calvin Lott, the Jefferson storekeeper, an unlikely visitor.

Twine went up front. Lott walked inside to meet him and said what he had made the long ride for. 'He's gone, Twine.'

'Who's gone?'

'Jess Bailey.'

Twine looked for something to sit on, saw several piled posts and sat on them regarding the store-keeper.

Lott didn't keep him waiting. 'Lucille Emory went to the parsonage lookin' for Jane Bailey. Neither one of 'em was there.' Lott made a slow study of the barn's interior. 'He couldn't have done it by himself . . . Is Jane here? She'd know.'

Twine was slowly recovering from his shock when he said, 'She's been here since early morning.'

'She hid him somewhere. You looked in the loft?'

Twine glanced at the loft ladder and arose. There was little possibility that a man could have carried Jess Bailey up that ladder, let alone a woman. He said, 'Look for yourself. Cal, I've been here all day. So has she.'

'But she rode out last night, late. The liveryman told me.'

Twine moved as far as the doorless wide barn opening and gazed in the direction of the house. It seemed as silent and shadowy as it had previously seemed.

He spoke without facing around. 'He was weak as a kitten last I saw him. Bled out and . . . ' He faced Lott. 'It wasn't her. How in hell could he even crawl as far as the door?'

Lott answered with dogged conviction. 'She helped him. Who else would've done it?'

'I just told you, she didn't help him, she left town late last night. That's what the liveryman told you, isn't it?'

'Yes, but . . . '

'Didn't he say she left alone?'

'No. All he said was that her horse was gone. He didn't see her leave.'

'An' you think she rode double with her brother?' Twine snorted. 'Use your head, Cal. Even if she could boost him behind the saddle in his condition he'd have fallen off before she covered half a mile.'

'I'd like to talk to her. Is she at the house?'

'She's at the house, but right now I don't think she'd want to talk to you.'

'You think she wouldn't. Why?'

Twine jerked his head, walked into the shadows, leaned and unrolled the top of the wagon canvas.

Cal Lott gasped. 'Wayne . . . ?'

Twine said nothing for a while, but eventually he explained that the elder Bailey had hanged himself last night which was the reason he didn't believe Jane or her sister should be subjected to questioning about their brother.

The storekeeper was badly shaken and turned away. Twine leaned to replace the covering canvas. Outside was dazzling daylight with almost endless visibility. Lott stopped just inside the wide doorway.

'He wouldn't have known anythin' about it, would he?'

Twine ignored the question when he spoke. 'Folks can stand just so much. He had his reasons. Jess was the biggest one.'

Lott turned. 'Then how in hell did he escape? He didn't come here unless his sister brought him.'

Twine looked dourly at the storekeeper. 'That is impossible an' it didn't happen,' he stated, enunciating very clearly.

'Then how'n hell did Bailey escape?'

'I got no idea. In his condition he couldn't have. If you find him, Cal, it won't be out here. You want to help me bury Wayne?'

Lott walked purposefully out to his horse, freed-up the reins, mounted, turned his back on Twine and started riding in the direction from which he had come.

Twine expectorated, watched the

storekeeper get small then returned to foraging for digging tools.

He had never dug a grave in his life. He had seen burials and had heard mention of the digging. It seemed graves were supposed to be four feet deep.

As he walked in the direction of the nearest big old tree west of the barn and corral he scuffed dirt expecting stone and found nothing but sod.

It was hot even in tree shade; by the time he was knee deep down he had to shed his shirt and had gone back to the trough for a long drink of cold water.

What he was doing was clearly visible from the house but he was not surprised that Wayne's girls did not appear.

By the time he thought the grave was deep enough, the sun was burnished copper off in the west.

He went back, hoisted the canvas bundle to his shoulder, carried it to the hole and knelt to gently lower it. He wasn't a praying man although in his childhood he'd been taught the Lord's

Prayer. He made an effort to recall it and repeated it then arose and went to work filling the grave.

By the time he was finished, dusk was fading into night and visibility went with it.

At the trough he stripped to the middle and washed in cold water. He was inside looking for something to dry off with when Jane appeared in the doorway, a leggy, solemn shadow carrying a tray.

As he towelled off on a crusty saddle blanket she took the tray to the pile of posts and put it down. When she turned she said, 'Supper . . . Twine, I'll never forget what I owe you.'

He went after his shirt and was buttoning it when he replied, 'You can make a marker, name, days of birth an' death.'

She nodded while saying she had no idea what her father's date of birth was.

He went to the tray and began to eat. She hovered. When he eventually told her why the storekeeper had ridden from town she put a hand to her mouth. Twine went on eating. After a long silence between them she said, 'How could he escape? How could he even crawl as far as the sick-room door?'

Twine chewed, swallowed and shook his head. 'That's what I told Lott.' He looked up. 'Maybe he could crawl to some hiding place, maybe the cellar or . . .'

'They'd search, Twine.'

That was true. He handed back the tray and said, 'I'll bed down in the loft. My back's hurtin'.'

'You bed down in the house. I'll rub some Sloan's Liniment on your back.'

He shook his head. 'I'll be fine come mornin'. I've slept in hay lofts before.' When she would have argued he held up an open hand.

She left with the tray and Twine considered the loft ladder which was one of those common ones made of a single log with braces spiked to it at intervals.

He went out back to listen to the night. Northward, invisible except for where the heights of Stone Mountain blocked out the stars he thought of his brother and his mother. If they had been able to stay together life probably wouldn't have been different than it had been for his mother and brother. He looked more Indian than Joe did.

Things that were set in stone when he'd been a child were less adhered to now but he was still a 'breed Indian.

He made no attempt to hide his feelings toward Jane Bailey. This far during their acquaintanceship she had proved to be what he expected in a woman.

Ruefully he smiled in the night. It took two to make a horse trade. So far she had given no indication that he could see of considering him anything more than what he was, a 'breed Indian wearing a white-man's badge,

217

living and thinking like a whiteskin.

Jane's sister was darker but right there any affinity ended. She had neither the strength nor toughness of Jane Bailey.

He considered the old cow in the corral, arose and told it, 'To hell with it,' and went to climb to the loft, and while that was something he'd done a hundred times without thinking, this time the climbing hit him in the back like a knotted scourage.

He climbed back down, leaned a moment then went searching among the stalls for a clean one with straw bedding, which he eventually found, went in, tossed down his hat, kicked out of his boots, looped his holstered Colt and shellbelt and used a rank old horse blanket as a covering and shifted around until he was comfortable and went to sleep.

Somewhere not too far out a wolf sounded. The next sound was of stampeding horses who had been closer to wherever that wolf had been.

Those horses could have stampeded

into the barn front and out the back and Twine Fourch would not have stirred.

If a man wanted exhaustive exercise he couldn't do any better than dig a grave and afterwards shovel it full.

12

Another Fatality

He might have slept past sunrise if a scrawny rooster in hot pursuit of an equally scrawny and harassed hen hadn't run across his stomach.

It was chilly. It usually was chilly before sunrise. He went out back to wash, marvelled that his facial hair had grown so flourishingly, went back inside to roll his blankets, saddle up, make the bedroll fast behind the cantle, lead the horse out and mount it.

Neither of them'd had any breakfast but Jefferson wasn't all that far.

Some animals were nocturnal hunters, some weren't, and still others hunted any time, dark or light. His horse abruptly changed leads without breaking its gait.

Twine peered into the predawn

gloom. Whatever had spooked his horse was out there and its presence upset it.

It is said horses are cowards, that they run from anything as negligible as an old scent. They aren't cowards; every animal has a defence mechanism, for horses it is flight. They are built for speed, it is their first line of defence, but if they can't flee they fight and a fighting horse is a formidable animal. He can fight with both ends; most animals can only fight with one end, their claws. A horse can strike in front with the speed of lightning.

Twine's animal began to subtly shift its weight to its hind legs. He peered hard between its ears, saw nothing, heard nothing and scented nothing.

Not until the bear came over a rolling rib of land and stopped dead still.

Twine felt the horse bunch to whirl and run. It would probably do the same thing if its rider fired a gun off its back. The choice was 'devil you do, devil you don't'.

Twine fisted his six-gun, reined to a halt leaving it up to the bear. It also stood its ground, not from belligerence but from total surprise at meeting a rider before daylight.

Twine aimed at the ground in front of the bear as he said, 'Well, you old bastard it's up to you.'

The bear shifted its feet and before firing Twine shortened his reins.

The explosion hurled dirt into the bear's face and sent it in a rippling pigeon-toed retreat.

The horse bunched under its saddle. Twine eased deeper and waited. The horse gradually came out of its poised position, shook its head for loose reins and started walking.

Twine looped his reins, shucked out the spent casing, plugged in a fresh load from his belt, leathered the weapon and unwound the reins. The crisis back there had been satisfactorily resolved.

Twine patted the horse's neck and told it for a moment back there he'd also been scairt peeless.

The chill increased until a streak of sickly colour appeared off in east then it began to lessen.

With Jefferson in sight, Twine wasn't surprised that only a few buildings showed lights. If he'd owned a watch he would have known it was something later than five in the morning.

He angled so as to cross the back alley behind the livery barn, dismounted out back and led his horse inside. Their arrival caused a stirring among other stalled animals, but neither the liveryman or his nighthawk appeared.

The liveryman was home in bed. His night man was sound asleep atop a pile of mostly salt-sweat-stiff saddle blankets.

Twine cared for the horse himself, walked up through to the roadway and looked in the direction of the eatery. It was dark.

Every business establishment including the saloon was dark. There was light coming past a window in the widow-woman's cottage, but he ignored that, crossed to the bench outside the emporium and sat, shoved out his legs, tipped down his hat and would have slept if someone inside the store hadn't rattled some chain and pulled back the roadway door.

The storekeeper looked southward then northward. He saw the town constable on his bench and didn't move for a long moment. Then he went over thinking Twine was asleep, and shook him.

Twine pushed off the shaking hand and stood up. 'I'm waitin' for pusgut to open his eatery,' he told Cal Lott, who stood staring at Twine. He jerked his head and led the way inside the store. Wordlessly he got a tin of peaches and a tin of sardines and put them in front of Twine at the counter. He then spoke his first words.

'When did you get back to town?'

Twine was digging for his clasp knife when he answered, 'Half-hour or so ago. What time is it?'

Lott ignored the question. 'You spent the night at the Bailey place?'

Twine had the tin of peaches open and was raising it when Lott spoke. He slowly lowered the can. 'That's where I spent the night. In a horse stall. Why?'

'Well, nothin', I just wondered. That'll be fifteen cents.'

After placing the coins on the counter-top Twine set his head slightly to one side. 'You feel all right?' he asked.

Lott showed life finally. 'Never felt better. Why, don't I look chipper?'

Twine drank syrup from the tin before answering. 'It's not that you look poorly, it's how you're acting. Is somethin' wrong? You found Jess Bailey?'

Lott looked toward the roadway door as though expecting customers to be standing there more than an hour before anyone would come shopping.

Twine emptied the peaches tin, wiped his mouth, put the tin of sardines in a shirt pocket and scowled. 'Cal . . . ?'

Lott turned back to face the constable. 'They found him.'

'Where was he? Hid?'

'Twine, I'd feel better if you asked up at the saloon.'

'The saloon's still locked up,' Twine stated, and leaned on the counter with an unwavering stare on the storekeeper. 'Cal, gawddammit!'

'You can't blame 'em, Twine. He killed a — '

'Cal, I'm goin' to come behind this counter and give you another lesson like I give you up yonder at that old cabin!'

Lot blurted it out. 'They hanged him.'

Twine neither lowered his eyes nor moved for a long moment before he slowly straightened up. 'Jess Bailey?'

'Twine, I had no idea. That's why I rode out yonder yesterday. I figured . . . '

'Who hanged him, Cal!'

226

'I don't know. I — most folks didn't know until Lucille was screamin' in the roadway in the dark. They took him out'n hanged him from one of them trees beside the road at the north end of town.'

'*Who, Cal!*'

'I told you, I didn't know they figured to do it. I don't know who done it. They cut him down an' buried him beside that other feller, the one named Carlile that they fetched back to town an' buried. I don't know who they was an' that's the gospel truth.'

Twine was a long time moving, but eventually he went out front. Now, there were more lights, mostly among residences, but as he stood out there with a new day breaking a light appeared in the saloon.

He went up there. He and the proprietor had been friends for years, but the proprietor was not there, a gangling, tow-headed man not yet out of his twenties was behind the bar. When Twine walked in the gangling man looked surprised. He told Twine the saloonman had left town several days back to go visit an ailing sister up in Laramie.

The gangling barman was nervous; he wiped the spotless bartop in the same place twice and creased his face into a fixed smile.

'Beer, Mr Fourch?'

Twine knew the temporary barman. His name was Hank Gilbert, he did odd jobs around the settlement. In fact, he was gifted with his hands, could make a five-drawer dresser as good as anything that was imported.

Folks didn't quite dislike Hank Gilbert, they were wary of him. For one thing he neither sparked local girls nor seemed comfortable among women. The Sioux had a name for the Hank Gilberts, it was *berdash*. No one in Jefferson had heard the word nor understood what it implied. They just were leery of a grown man who played tag with the children and carved things for them.

On his second sweep of the bartop, Twine reached, caught his arm and said, 'Did you help 'em pull Jess Bailey up?'

The shockle-headed man tried to jerk his arm clear as he spoke. 'I . . . was home asleep . . . but I helped dig the grave. Least a person can do, Constable.'

Twine's grip tightened. 'Who were they, Hank?'

'I told you, I was asleep in bed.'

'How'd you come to help dig the grave?'

'Well, it was the Christian thing to do.'

Twine released his grip. 'How many was there?'

'Four.'

'You saw four men an' didn't recognize any of 'em?'

'I told you — '

It wasn't a blow it was an open-handed slap. 'I'll break your neck, Hank!'

'Two of 'em was rangemen. They

229

was in the saloon when the other two come in an' talked to 'em. The four of 'em left. One was the stage-yard boss.'

'Justin Abbot?'

'Yes. Him. The other one was Jack Henley, Mister Abbot's foreman at the corralyard.'

'Who were the rangemen?'

'I don't know. I don't recollect ever seein' either of 'em before.'

Twine left the saloon walking in the direction of the corralyard. It was between time for getting stages ready. Two Mexican-looking hostlers were in shade soaping harness. They were affable until Twine asked where Jack Henley was, then they both shrugged; they didn't know where the yard boss was.

Twine went to the office which had two doors; one opened into the yard the other door opened on the road.

Justin Abbot was working amid a litter of papers at a desk. When he looked up, saw Twine, he tossed a pencil aside and leaned back. He offered no greeting, just waited.

It was a short wait. Twine stood across from Abbot at his desk and spoke without preliminaries. 'What in the hell were you thinkin' of? All you fellers had to do was wait. His chance of recoverin' was down to zero.'

Abbot gazed dispassionately at his visitor and offered a chair, which Twine declined before the corralyard boss said, 'You'd've done the same thing if you wasn't wearin' that badge. Did you know that miserable son of a bitch shot an' killed a woman an' a kid up north?'

Abbot rocked forward to lean on his littered desk. 'Their name was Alford. It was the woman's brother an' her husband. They went manhuntin' and got this far. We was at the saloon when they come in an' asked about Bailey an' Carlile by name . . . they told us what them two had done up north.'

Abbot picked up the pencil and

balanced it between the first fingers of each hand. 'Twine, you knew Jess Bailey. So did everyone else. A worthless, lyin', thievin', murderin' son of a bitch. It didn't take much . . . we dragged him out and hung him.'

Twine accepted the chair, sat down and looked steadily at the corralyard boss. 'His pa hanged himself night before last in his barn.'

Abbot let the pencil drop. 'Old Wayne? I knew him well, nice, honest feller. I'm sorry to hear it.' Abbot paused. 'Then he didn't know what happened to his son. Just as well. He's had his share of heart-breaks, he didn't need another one.'

Twine shoved his legs out and loosened in the chair. 'You know lynchin' can get you ten years in prison.'

Abbot picked up the pencil and balanced it again without looking at Twine. 'There's no judge or jury in the territory that'll hand down a hard judgement for what we done an' you know it.'

'Where's Henley?'

'He went up country with the wagon an' an extra wheel. We got a broken-down stage up near the Stone Mountain turnoff.' Abbot raised his eyes. 'Twine, we wasn't drinkin'. Well, not barely. When those cowmen walked in lookin' for Jess Bailey and told us why . . . ' Abbot dropped the pencil and leaned back off the desk. 'Twine, I told 'em Jess would sure as hell die. All they had to do was wait. You know what the woman's husband said to me? 'My boy was thirteen years old. My wife was the sweetest, finest woman I ever knew. We didn't do all this manhuntin' to wait for that bastard to die. Put yourself in our boots'.'

Abbot paused again. 'My yard foreman remembered somethin' like that happenin' down in Texas. He said the four of us ought to take that no-good son of a bitch out an' hang him.'

Twine said, 'An' you went along?'

233

Justin Abbot nodded. 'An' I went along.'

Twine arose and reset his hat and got as far as the roadway door before Abbot spoke. 'You want to arrest me'n my yard foreman?'

Twine passed through the door as though he had heard nothing, closed the door and walked the half-mile to the Jefferson graveyard. He couldn't miss the pair of graves, they were the only fresh ones. Each had a headboard with a name and the date of death on it and that was all.

On his way back to the jailhouse he was struck with a stunning thought. If Jane rode to town. No, *when* she rode to town.

He went down to get his horse and, as before, the usually garrulous liveryman would neither look him in the eye or speak.

Ordinarily he considered the ride out yonder to take an inordinate length of time. Not today. He breasted the low slope where he'd encountered the bear in what seemed a short ride.

There was smoke rising from the Bailey ranch's main house but no one was in sight. The 'doctored' cow was eating from a flake of hay and except for watching him alight and tie up paid no attention. Twine barely glanced out back or he would have noticed that the cow was no longer shaking her head.

There was a top buggy with a bay mare between the shafts tied up at the rack in front of the house. Top buggies had a very little box behind the seat for carrying supplies from town. The storage space was too limited for much else.

Twine stopped. The area behind the seat had two heavy satchels and several boxes tightly tied, all the box could hold.

In anticipation of what this signified, when Twine knocked on the door he removed his hat.

Jane faced him, stepped aside and, without speaking, left him standing in the parlour. From somewhere in the back of the house he could hear Jane and her sister talking.

The old framed picture of Wayne and his wife was gone as were several other personal items.

Jane returned and offered coffee. Twine shook his head. She studied his face. 'Jess?'

He nodded.

'When?'

'Night before last.'

Jane looked away then back. 'I thought so. He'd bled a lot.'

Twine gazed out the window as he said, 'Take a walk with me.'

They left the house and she set her pace to his slower gait. He neither spoke nor slowed at the barn, but kept on walking until they were beyond the yard and its buildings. Then he chose a shade tree and told her to sit down.

She remained standing. 'Twine?'

'Did you know Jess killed a ranch woman an' her thirteen-year-old son up north?'

She remained facing him, made no

effort to sit. 'Jess and John?'

'Well no, not Carlile, Jess.' He paused before telling her the rest. 'The woman's husband an' her brother got on their trail an' ended up in Jefferson.'

'And . . . ?'

'Sure you don't want to sit down?'

'They killed Jess.'

He nodded. 'Lynched him.'

She sank down in tree shade. He sat close by. 'A couple of townsmen helped. Folks cut him down an' buried him beside Carlile.'

A woman's call from the yard was distinguishable but barely. 'Jane, you know where I'll be.'

They sat in silence as Jane's sister lined out the buggy horse and drove southward. Jane spoke in a leaden voice. 'She's going down to our Aunt Clara's place in Texas.' Jane stood up and dusted off. 'I'll be leaving too. I'll take the buckboard. My sorrel mare's broke to drive.'

He got up facing her. Her eyes were

dry, but if a facial expression was capable of mirroring a broken heart, Jane Bailey's did.

'You got livestock, Jane, some cows an' horses.'

'Twine, you can have them. And the ranch. Wild horses couldn't make me stay here. I'll never enter that barn again as long as I live.' She paused to sniffle then spoke on a subject which was foreign. She said, 'I'll never set foot in Pineville or Jefferson again. Let's walk back.'

Twine Fourch had never been a talkative person and right now as they walked side by side he felt more tongue-tied than ever before, until they were near the porch steps, then he spoke.

'Where'll you go?'

She looked past him northward where it was not difficult to make out the beak and eyes of the eagle on Stone Mountain. 'I think I'll go up yonder.' She brought her gaze back to his face. 'Do you know who owns maybe a section of land up there?'

'I don't know but I can find out. As worthless as that country is it's likely on the unclaimed homestead lists. Why up there?'

'I like that kind of country; it's wild and free without people.'

'Jane, that house up there's ready to fall down.'

She startled him with her smile. 'I'll build another one.' The smile winked out. 'I'll take tools. You can have the ranch and what goes with it. If you want a quit claim ride up and I'll sign it.'

'Jane, what would I do with your ranch? I'm not a — '

'Sell it. Buy a house in town. You want to help me load the buckboard?'

He nodded dumbly, didn't say ten words until the wagon was loaded and she was evening up the lines on the seat. Then, when she smiled down at him, he said, 'How soon can I come up an' help you? Maybe my brother . . . '

'Your brother is a loner. He wouldn't

239

like anyone settling in up there.'

That was probably true. Twine stepped back to avoid the rear wheels and smiled at her. She didn't slap the lines so the sorrel mare didn't move.

'I owe you an awful lot, Twine.'

For once the right words came. 'We could talk about that up yonder when we're buildin' your house.'

She talked up the sorrel mare, drove out of the yard without looking back, not even to wave.

He waited until he could no longer see wagon dust then headed for Jefferson and didn't arrive until evening was darkening along toward full night.

It was close enough to supper-time for the settlement to be well lighted, several stores were serving customers. Cal Lott's general store, with fewer patrons, was in process of closing for the day. Between the time Twine left his horse at the livery barn and walked up to the jailhouse, the last lights in the emporium had been extinguished.

He lighted the overhead lamp, sat

behind his table and barely heard or noticed the sounds around him until Justin Abbot walked in, nodded, took a chair and said, 'Alford an' his brother-in-law left. We shared a drink at the saloon then they left. Twine, you're the local law . . .'

Twine understood the implication and dropped his hat on the table as he said, 'I rode out to the Bailey place today. Justin, tellin' them how their brother died was the hardest thing I ever did in my life.'

Abbot remained quiet, on this subject there was nothing for him to say.

'You want to know if I'm goin' after Alford? No; you want to know why? Because Jess Bailey wasn't worth the effort of finding them fellers an' bringin' them back. Except for Jess Bailey none of this would have happened. As far as I'm concerned, it's ended. Do you by any chance know who owns the land up yonder where that old cabin sets?'

'Far as I know it's government land. Why; you want it?'

'Someone does.'

'I got to go down yonder soon, I can stop by the government land office an' find out.'

'I'd appreciate that, Justin. How did Jess die?'

'While we was draggin' him out to the tree, the son of a bitch passed out. He hung up there limp as a rag.' Justin arose. 'You had supper?'

Twine lied with a clear conscience. 'A while back.'

When the corralyard boss left, Twine groped for his bottle of pop skull, took one long drink and put the bottle back in its dark place.

For the next few days he wasn't exactly avoided but neither was he greeted with the friendly casualness of former days. The next time he met Justin Abbot, the corralyard boss spread a wrinkled map and pointed to a section of land someone had outlined in dark pencil. 'It's up for a homestead claim,' he said. 'The clerk down there asked me who in hell would want such a worthless piece of land.'

'What did you tell him?'

'That I didn't know,' Abbot replied, as he headed for the door. With the door open, he also said, 'An' that's the gospel truth.'

The following week, Twine rode down to the territorial land office, filed on two 160-acre parcels, paid the fee and rode back to Jefferson. He was unable to leave Jefferson again until the end of the following week when he left the settlement a couple of hours before sunrise and arrived on the small clearing with its sag-roofed old log house in time for Jane to invite him to breakfast.

It was a Spartan meal and Twine ate everything in sight. As Jane already knew he either had worms or a hollow leg.

She showed him where she had rebuilt the old rock corral where her sorrel mare eyed them with an expression of curiosity and indifference.

While they were at the restored corral

he handed her the homestead papers. She read them and without warning threw herself against him and kissed him squarely on the mouth. If he'd ever been kissed like that before he would have remembered it. He hadn't.

They went around where she had used the sorrel mare to snake delimbed and draw-knifed logs to the stump area behind the house.

He said, 'Roof rafters?'

'Yes. Roof rafters first, then . . . '

'Jane, this isn't woman's work.'

'You might be right. You got any idea where I can get a big stout man to help?'

At the expression on his face she laughed. After a moment he also laughed. As they were walking toward the cabin she said, 'What'll folks think, you coming up here and helping me?'

'I never would've thought of that. Would it bother you?'

'Not a bit.'

He gazed in the direction of the corral. 'Does your mare pack?'

'She'll do anything a person wants. She'll pack. Why?'

'Let's go inside. You make up a list of what's goin' to be needed. I'll take the mare back with me, borrow a pack outfit and come back.'

They entered the old house. It had been cleaned and swept out. He said, 'First off you'll need an axe an' matches.'

'I have them, but maybe a few sticks of dynamite to blow out the stumps an' make a stone fence around a pasture.'

'You got a pencil?'

THE END

RIDERS OF RIFLE RANGE
Wade Hamilton

Veterinarian Jeff Jones did not like open warfare — but it was there on Scrub Pine grass. When he diagnosed a sick bull on the Endicott ranch as having the contagious blackleg disease, he got involved in the warfare — whether he liked it or not!

BEAR PAW
Nevada Carter

Austin Dailey traded two cows to a pair of Indians for a bay horse, which subsequently disappeared. Tracks led to a secret hideout of fugitive Indians — and cattle thieves. Indians and stockmen co-operated against the rustlers. But it was Pale Woman who acted as interpreter between her people and the rangemen.

THE WEST WITCH
Lance Howard
Detective Quinton Hilcrest journeys west, seeking the Black Hood Bandits' lost fortune. Within hours of arriving in Hags Bend, he is fighting for his life, ensnared with a beautiful outcast the town claims is a witch! Can he save the young woman from the angry mob?

GUNS OF THE PONY EXPRESS
T. M. Dolan
Rich Zennor joined the Pony Express venture at the start, as second-in-command to tough Denning Hartman. But Zennor had the problems of Hartman believing that they had crossed trails in the past, and the fact that he was strongly attached to Hartman's Indian girl, Conchita.

BLACK JO OF THE PECOS
Jeff Blaine

Nobody knew where Black Josephine Callard came from or whither she returned. Deputy U.S. Marshal Frank Haggard would have to exercise all his cunning and ability to stay alive before he could defeat her highly successful gang and solve the mystery.

RIDE FOR YOUR LIFE
Johnny Mack Bride

They rode west, hoping for a new start. Then they met another broken-down casualty of war, and he had a plan that might deliver them from despair. But the only men who would attempt it would be the truly brave — or the desperate. They were both.

NEATH PORT TALBOT LIBRARY AND INFORMATION SERVICES

1	12/06	25		49		73	
2		26		50		74	
3		27	9/08	51		75	
4	8/03	28		52		76	
5		29		53		77	
6		30	7/05	54		78	
7	5/01	31		55		79	12/06
8	9/00	32		56		80	
9	12/09	33	10/15	57		81	
10		34		58		82	
11		35		59		83	
12		36		60		84	
13		37		61		85	
14		38		62		86	
15		39	3/15	63		87	
16		40		64		88	
17		41		65		89	
18		42		66		90	
19		43		67		91	
20		44		68		92	
21	6/15	45	6/24	69		COMMUNITY SERVICES	
22		46		70			
23		47		71		NPT/111	
24		48		72			